ITALIAN'S BABY

BY
LUCY GORDON

MILLS & BOON®

First published in Great Britain 2003
Harlequin Mills & Boon Limited,
Eton House, 18-24 Paradise Road, Richmond, Surrey TW9 1SR

© Lucy Gordon 2003

ISBN 0 263 17780 7

Set in Times Roman 10½ on 12¼ pt.
07-1003-44632

Printed and bound in Great Britain
by Antony Rowe Ltd, Chippenham, Wiltshire

PROLOGUE

She was seventeen, as pretty as a doll, and as lifeless, sitting in the window, staring out, unseeing, over the Italian countryside.

She didn't turn when the door opened and a nurse came in, with a middle-aged man. He had an air of joviality that sat oddly with his cold eyes.

'How's my best girl?' he greeted the doll by the window.

She neither replied nor looked at him.

'I've got someone to see you, precious.' He turned to a young man standing behind him and said curtly, 'Make it quick.'

He was twenty, little more than a boy. His hair was shaggy, he looked as though he hadn't shaved for days, and his eyes were wild with pain and anger. He went quickly to the girl and dropped on his knees beside her, speaking in an imploring voice.

'Becky, *mia piccina*—it is I, Luca. Look at me, I beg you. Forgive me for everything—they say our child is dead and that it is my fault—I never meant to hurt you—can you hear me?'

She turned her head and seemed to look at him, but there was no recognition in her eyes. They were lifeless.

'Listen to me,' the boy implored. 'I am sorry, *piccina,* I am so sorry. Becky, for pity's sake, say that you understand.'

5

She was silent. He reached up a hand to brush her light brown hair aside. She did not move.

'I did not see our baby,' he said huskily. 'Was she pretty like you? Did you hold her? Speak to me. Tell me that you know me, that you love me still. I shall love you all my life. Only say that you forgive me for all the pain I have brought you. I meant only to make you happy. *In God's name, speak to me.*'

But she said nothing, merely stared out of the window. He dropped his head into her lap, and the only sound in the room was his sobs.

CHAPTER ONE

THE words stood out starkly, black against the white paper.

A boy. Born yesterday. 8lbs 6oz.

A simple message that might have been the bringer of joy. But to Luca Montese it meant that his wife had given a son to another man, and none to him. It meant that the world would know of his humiliation, and that made him curse until there was nobody left to curse, except himself, for being a blind fool. His face was not pleasant at that moment. It was cruel and frightening.

Fear of that face had made Drusilla leave him as soon as she knew she was pregnant, six months ago. He had arrived home to find her gone, leaving him a note. It had said that there was another man. She was pregnant. It was no use trying to find her. That was all.

She had taken everything he had ever given her, down to the last diamond, the last stitch of couture clothing. He'd pursued her like an avenging fury, not in person but through a battery of expensive lawyers, nailing her down to a divorce settlement that left her nothing beyond what she had already taken.

It galled him that the man was so poor and insignificant as to be virtually beyond the reach of his revenge. If he had been a rich entrepreneur, like himself, it would have been a pleasure to ruin him. But a hairdresser! That was the final insult.

Now they had a big, lusty son. And Luca Montese was childless. The world would know that it was his fault that his marriage had been barren, and the world would laugh. The thought almost drove him to madness.

Three floors below him was the heart of Rome's financial district, a world he had made his own by shrewdness, cunning and sheer brute muscle. His employees were in awe of him, his rivals were afraid of him. That was how he liked it. But now they would laugh.

He turned the paper between his fingers. His hands were heavy and strong, the hands of a workman, not an international financier.

His face was the same; blunt-featured, with a heaviness about it that had little to do with the shape of features, and more to do with a glowering intensity in his eyes. That, and his tall, broad-shouldered body, attracted the kind of woman—and there were plenty of them—who gravitated towards power. Physical power. Financial power. All kinds. Since the break-up of his marriage he hadn't lacked company.

He treated them well, according to his lights, was generous with gifts but not with words or feelings, and broke with them abruptly when he realised they did not have what he was seeking.

He could not have said what that was. He only knew that he'd found it once, long ago, with a girl who had shining eyes and a great heart.

He barely remembered the boy he'd been then, full of impractical ideas about love lasting forever. Not cynical, not grasping, believing that love and life were both good: a foolishness that had been cruelly cured.

He brought himself firmly back to the present. Dwelling on lost happiness was a weakness, and he always cut out weakness as ruthlessly as he did everything else. He strode out of the office and down to the underground parking lot, where his Rolls-Royce—this year's model—was waiting.

He had a chauffeur but he loved driving it himself. It was his personal trophy, the proof of how far he'd come since the days when he'd had to make do with an old jalopy that would have collapsed if he hadn't repaired it himself.

Even with his best efforts it was liable to break down at odd moments, and then *she* would laugh and chatter as she handed him spanners. Sometimes she would get under the car with him, and they would kiss and laugh like mad things.

And perhaps it was a kind of madness, he thought as he headed the Rolls out of Rome to his villa in the country. Mad, because that heart-stopping joy could never last. And it hadn't.

He'd brushed the thought of her aside once, but now she seemed to be there beside him as he drove on in the darkness, tormenting him with memories of how enchanting she had been, with her sweet gentleness, her tenderness, her endless giving. He had been twenty, and she seventeen, and they'd thought it would last forever.

Perhaps it might have done if—

He shut off that thought too. Strong man though he was, the 'what if?' was unbearable.

But her ghost wouldn't be banished. It whispered sadly that their brief love had been perfect, even though it had ended in heartbreak. She reminded him of other things too, how she'd lain in his arms, whispering words of love and passion.

'I'm yours, always—always—I shall never love any other man—'

'I have nothing to offer you—'

'If you give me your love, that's all I ask.'

'But I'm a poor man.'

How she had laughed at that, ripples of young, confident laughter that had filled his soul. 'We're not poor—as long as we have each other...'

And then it was over, and they no longer had each other.

Suddenly there was a squeal of tyres and the wheel spun in his hand. He didn't know what had happened, except that the car had stopped and he was shaking.

He got out to clear his head, looking up and down the country road. It was empty in both directions.

Like his life, he thought. Coming out of the empty darkness and leading ahead into empty darkness.

It had been that way for fifteen years.

The Allingham was the newest, most luxurious hotel to have gone up in London's exclusive Mayfair. Its service was the best, its prices the highest.

Rebecca Hanley had been appointed its first PR consultant partly because, as the chairman of the board had said, 'She looks as if she grew up with money to burn, and didn't give a damn. And that's useful when you're trying to get people to burn money without giving a damn.'

Which was astute of him, because Rebecca's father had been a very rich man indeed. And these days she didn't give a damn about anything.

She lived in the Allingham, because it was simpler than having a home of her own. She used the hotel's beauty salon and gymnasium, and the result was a figure that wasn't an ounce overweight, and a face that was a mask of perfection.

Tonight she was putting the final touches to her appearance when the phone rang. It was Danvers Jordan, the banker who was her current escort.

They were to attend the engagement party of his younger brother, held in the Allingham. As Danvers' companion and a representative of the hotel, she would be 'on duty' in two ways, and must look right, down to every detail.

As she checked herself in three angled mirrors Rebecca knew that nobody could fault her looks. She had the slim, elegant body that could wear the tight black dress, and the endless legs demanded by the short skirt. The neckline was low-cut, but within relatively modest limits. Around her neck she wore one large diamond.

Her hair had started life as light brown, but now it was a soft honey-blonde that struck a strange, distinctive note with her green eyes. Small diamonds in her ears added the final touch.

On exactly the stroke of eight the knock came on her door and she sauntered gracefully across to let Danvers in.

'You look glorious,' he said, as he always did. 'I shall be the proudest man there.'

Proudest. Not happiest.

The party was in a banqueting room, hung with drapes of white silk interspersed with masses of white roses. The engaged couple were little more than children, Rory twenty-four, Elspeth eighteen. Elspeth's father was the president of the merchant bank for which Danvers worked, and which was part of the consortium that had financed the Allingham.

She was like a kitten, Rebecca thought, sweet, innocent and intense about everything, especially being in love.

'I didn't think people talked about "forever and ever" any more,' she said to Danvers when the evening was half over.

'I suppose if you're young enough and stupid enough it seems to make sense,' he said wryly.

'Do you really have to be young and stupid?'

'Come on, darling! Grown-ups know that things happen, life goes wrong.'

'That's true,' she said quietly.

Elspeth came flying up to them, throwing her arms around Rebecca.

'Oh, I'm so happy. And what about you two? It's time you tied the knot. Why don't we make the announcement now?'

'No,' Rebecca said quickly. Then, fearing that she had been too emphatic, she hastened to add, 'This is your night. If I hijacked it I'd be in trouble with my boss.'

'All right, but on my wedding day I'm going to toss you my bouquet.'

She danced away and Rebecca heaved a secret sigh of relief.

'Why did she call you Becky?' Danvers asked.

'It's short for Rebecca.'

'I've never heard anyone use it with you, and I'm glad. Rebecca's more natural to you, gracious and sophisticated. You're not a Becky sort of person.'

'And what is "a Becky sort of person" Danvers?'

'Well, a bit coltish and awkward. Somebody who's just a kid and doesn't know much about the world.'

She put her glass down suddenly because her hand was shaking. But she knew he wouldn't notice.

'I haven't always been gracious and sophisticated,' she said.

'That's how I like to see you, though.'

And, of course, Danvers wouldn't be interested in any other version of her than the one that suited himself. She would probably marry him in the end, not for love, but for lack of any strong opposing force. She was thirty-two and the aimless drift that was her life couldn't go on indefinitely.

She rejected his suggestion of dinner, claiming tiredness. He saw her to her suite and made one last attempt to prolong the evening, drawing her close for a practiced kiss, but she stiffened.

'I really am very tired. Goodnight, Danvers.'

'All right. You get your beauty sleep and be perfect for tomorrow.'

'Tomorrow?'

'We're having dinner with the chairman of the bank. You can't have forgotten.'

'Of course not. I'll be there, at my best. Goodnight.'

If he didn't go soon she would scream.

At last she had the blessed relief of solitude. She turned out the lights and went to stand in the window, looking out at the lights of London. They winked and glittered against the darkness, and in her morbid mood it seemed as if she was looking at her whole life from now on: an endless vista of shiny occasions—dinner with the chairman, a box at the opera, lunch in fashionable restaurants, entertaining in a luxurious house, the perfect wife and hostess.

It had seemed enough before, but something about tonight had unsettled her. That young couple with their passionate belief in love had reminded her of too many things she no longer believed.

'Becky' had believed them, but Becky was dead. She had died in a confusion of pain, misery and disillusion.

Yet tonight her ghost had walked through the costly feast, turning reproachful eyes on Rebecca, reminding her that once she had had a heart, and had given that heart freely to a wild-eyed young man who had adored her.

'A kid, who doesn't know much about the world,' had been Danvers' verdict on 'Becky', and he was more right than he knew. They had both been kids, herself and the twenty-year-old, Luca, thinking that their love was the final answer to all problems.

Becky Solway had fallen in love with Italy at first sight, and especially the land around Tuscany, where her father had inherited the estate of Belleto from his Italian mother.

'Dad, it's heavenly!' she said when she first saw it. 'I want to stay here forever and ever.'

He laughed. 'All right, pet. Whatever you say.'

He was like that, always willing to indulge her without actually considering what she was saying, much less what she was thinking or feeling.

At fourteen all she saw was the indulgence. It had been just the two of them since her mother had died two years before. Frank Solway, successful manufacturer of electronic products, and his bright, pretty daughter.

He had factories all over Europe, continually moving the work to wherever the labour was cheapest. During her school vacation they travelled together, visiting the outposts of his business empire, or stayed at Belleto. The rest of the time she finished her schooling in England. When she was sixteen she announced that she was finished with school.

'I just want to live at Belleto from now on, Dad.'

And, as always, he said, 'All right, pet. Whatever you like.'

He bought her a horse, and she spent happy days exploring the vineyards and olive groves that formed part of Belleto's riches.

She had a quick ear, and had learned not only Italian from her grandmother but also the local Tuscan dialect. Her father spoke languages badly and the servants who ran his house found him hard to understand, so he soon left the domestic affairs to her. After a while she was helping with the estate as well.

All she knew of Frank was that he was a successful businessman. She never suspected a darker side, until one day it was forced on her.

He had closed his last factory in England, opened another in Italy, then taken off for Spain, inspecting new premises. During his absence Becky went for a ride and found herself confronted by three grim-faced men.

'You're Solway's daughter,' said one of the men in English. 'Frank Solway is your dad. Admit it.'

'Why should I deny it? I'm not ashamed of my father.'

'Well, you damned well should be,' another man shouted. 'We needed our jobs and he shut down the English factory overnight because it's cheaper over here.

No compensation, no redundancy. He just vanished. Where is he?'

'My father's abroad at the moment. Please let me pass.'

One of the men grabbed the bridle. 'Tell us where he is,' he snapped. 'We didn't come all this way to be fobbed off.'

She was growing nervous, sensing that they would soon be out of control.

'He'll be next week,' she said desperately. 'I'll tell him you called; I'm sure he'll want to speak to you—'

This brought a roar of ribald laughter.

'We're the last people he wants to speak to—he's been hiding from us...won't answer letters.'

'But what can I do?' she cried.

'You can stay with us until he comes for you,' the most unpleasant-looking man snapped, still holding the bridle.

'I think not,' said a hard voice.

It came from a young man that nobody had noticed. He had appeared from between the trees and stood still for a moment to make sure they had registered his presence. It was an impressive presence, not so much for his height and breadth of shoulder as for the sheer ferocity on his face.

'Stand back,' he said, starting to move forward.

'Get out of here,' said the man holding the bridle.

The stranger wasted no further words. Turning almost casually, he made a movement too fast to see, and the next moment the man was on the ground.

''Ere...' said one of the others.

But his words died unspoken as the stranger scowled at him.

'Leave here, all of you,' he said sternly. 'Do not come back.'

The other two hastened to help their companion to his feet. He was trying to staunch the blood from his nose and although the look he cast his assailant was furious he was too wise to take the matter further. He let himself be led away, but he turned at the last moment to glare back at Becky in a way that made the young man start forward. Then they all scuttled away.

'Thank you,' said Becky fervently.

'Are you all right?' he demanded abruptly.

'Yes, thanks to you.'

She dismounted, and immediately realised just how tall he was. Now his grim face and dark, intense eyes were looking down at her, the traces of cold rage still visible.

The angry little crowd had been alarming because there were three of them. But this man was dangerous on his own account, and suddenly she wondered if she was any safer than before.

'They've gone now,' he said. 'They won't come back.'

It was a simple statement of fact. He knew nobody would choose to face him twice.

'Thank you,' she said, speaking English, as he had done, but slowly. 'I've never been so glad to see anyone. I thought there was nobody to help me.'

'You don't have to speak slowly,' he said proudly. 'I know English.'

'I'm sorry. I didn't mean to be rude. Where did you appear from?'

'I live just past those trees. You had better come with me, and I will make you some tea.'

'Thank you.'

As they walked he said, 'I know everybody around here, but I've never seen them before.'

'They come from England. They were looking for my father, but he's away and that made them angry.'

'Perhaps you should not have ridden alone.'

'I didn't know they were there, and why shouldn't I ride where I like on my father's land?'

'Ah, yes, your father is the Englishman everyone is talking of. But this is not his land. It belongs to me. Just a narrow strip, but it contains my home, which I will not sell.'

'But Dad told me...' She checked herself.

'He told you that he'd bought all the land round here. He must have overlooked this little piece. It's very easily done.'

'Oh, that's lovely,' she said involuntarily.

They had turned a corner and come across a small stone cottage. It nestled against the lee of a hill in the shadow of pine trees, and her first thought was that it looked cosy and welcoming.

'It is my home,' he said simply. 'I warn you, it is not so picturesque inside.'

He spoke the truth. The inside was shabby and basic, with flagstones on the floor and a huge old-fashioned range. He was evidently working hard at improving it, for there were tools lying about, and planks of wood.

'Sit down,' he said, indicating a wooden chair that looked hard but turned out to be surprisingly comfortable.

There was a kettle on the range, and he made tea efficiently.

'I don't know your name,' she said.

'I am Luca Montese.'

'I'm Rebecca Solway. Becky.'

He looked down at the small, elegant hand she held out to him. For the first time he seemed to become uncertain. Then he thrust out his own hand. It was coarse and powerful, bruised and battered by heavy work. It engulfed hers out of sight.

His whole appearance was rough. His dark hair needed cutting and hung shaggily about his thickly muscled neck. He wore worn black jeans and a black sleeveless vest, and he was well over six feet, built on impressive lines.

Hercules, she thought.

The frightening rage in his face had disappeared entirely now, and the look he turned on her was gentle, although unsmiling. 'Rebecca,' he repeated.

'No, Becky to my friends. You are my friend, aren't you? You must be, after you saved me.'

For the whole of her short life, her charm and beauty had won people over. It was unusual for anyone not to warm to her easily, but she could sense this young man's hesitation.

'Yes,' he said awkwardly at last. 'I am your friend.'

'Then you'll call me Becky?'

'Becky.'

'Do you live here alone, or with a family?'

'I have no family. This was my mother's and father's house, and now it belongs to me.'

The firm tone in which he said the last words prompted her to say, 'Hey, I'm not arguing about that. It's yours, it's yours.'

'I wish your father felt the same way. Where is he now?'

'In Spain. He'll be home next week.'

'Until then I think it's better if you don't ride alone.'

She had been thinking the same thing, but this easy assumption of authority riled her.

'I beg your pardon?'

He frowned. 'There is no need to beg my pardon.'

'No, that's not what I meant,' she said, realising that his English was not as good as he'd claimed. '"I beg your pardon" is an expression that means "Who the heck do you think you are to give me orders?".'

He frowned again. 'Then why not just say so?'

'Because...' But the task of explaining was too much. She abandoned English in favour of Tuscan dialect.

'Don't give me orders. I'll ride as I please.'

'And what happens next time, when I may not be there to come to your aid?' he asked in the same language.

'They'll have gone by now.'

'And if you're wrong?'

'That's—that's got nothing to do with it,' she floundered, unable to counter the argument.

A faint smile appeared on his face. 'I think it has.'

'Oh, stop being so reasonable!' she said crossly.

The smile became a grin. 'Very well. Whatever pleases you.'

She smiled back ruefully. 'You might be right.'

He refilled her cup and she sipped it appreciatively. 'You make very good tea. I'm impressed.'

'And *I* am impressed that you speak my dialect so well.'

'My grandmother taught me. She came from here. She used to own the house where we live now.'

'Emilia Talese?'

'That was her maiden name, yes.'

'My family have always been carpenters. They used to do jobs for *her* family.'

That was their first meeting. He walked home with her, coming into the house, instructing the servants to take good care of her, as if he'd been commanding people all his life.

'Will you be all right?' she asked, thinking of him walking back alone in the gathering dusk. 'Suppose they're waiting for you?'

His grin was answer enough. It said that such fears were for other men. Then he walked out, leaving behind only the memory of his brilliant self-confidence. It was as strong as sunlight, and he seemed both to carry it with him, and leave it behind wherever he had been.

CHAPTER TWO

NEXT day Becky left the house early and rode down to find him. She had gone to bed thinking of him, lain awake thinking of him, finally slept, dreaming of him, then awoke thinking of him. She saw his face, young yet forceful, the mouth that was too stern for his years, until he smiled and became suddenly charming.

His mouth haunted her. With everything in her she wanted to kiss it, and to feel it kissing her back. And his arms, as powerful as steel hawsers, belonged around her. She knew that, as certainly as she had ever known anything, knew it with the conviction of a girl who had never seriously been denied anything she really wanted.

She had never even kissed a man before. But now that she'd met Luca she wanted him completely, in every way. It was as though her body had come alive in an instant, sending a message to her brain: this is the one.

The only question was how and when. It was impossible that the world, or Luca himself, could deny her.

As she approached he heard the hoof beats and looked up. She jumped down from the horse, facing him, and she knew at once, with joyful certainty, that he too had lain awake all night. But he turned away from her.

'You shouldn't be here,' he said. 'I told you not to ride alone.'

'Then why didn't you come for me?'

'Because the *signorina* did not give me orders to do so,' he said proudly.

'But I don't give you orders. We're just friends.'

She stood looking into his face, willing him to let her have her wish. He gave the slow smile that already made her heart beat strongly.

'Why don't you go and make the tea?' he suggested.

She did so, and spent the rest of the day helping him work on the house. He made rolls with salami, which was the most delicious food she'd ever tasted. But she hadn't given up her determination to make him kiss her. Sooner or later he would yield.

It took her three days to crack his resistance. During that time she came to know the man a little. He had a touchy pride that could make his temper smoulder, although he always reined it in quickly for her sake.

On the first day he had said, 'Whatever pleases you,' and that became his mantra. Whatever pleased her was right for him. This big man, who could be so ferocious to others, was like a child in her hands. It gave her a delicious sense of power.

But she couldn't make him do the one thing she wanted above all else. She created chance after chance, and he wouldn't take any of them, until one day he said, 'I think you should go home now.' He added in slow, awkward English, 'It has been very nice knowing you.'

Her answer was to pick up a bread roll from the table and hurl it at him. He ducked, but didn't seem disconcerted.

'Why don't you like me any more?' she cried.

'I do like you, Becky. I like you more than I should. That is why you must go, and not come back.'

'That doesn't make any sense!'

'I think you know just what I mean.'

'No!' she cried, refusing to understand what didn't suit her.

'I think you do. You know what I want with you, and I can't have it. I *must* not. You're a child.'

'I'm seventeen. Well, I will be in a couple of weeks. I'm *not* a child.'

'You talk like one. What you want, you must have. For the moment you want me, but I'm a man, not a toy to be played with then cast aside.'

'I'm not playing.'

'But you are. You're like a kitten with a cotton reel. You haven't yet learned that life can be cruel and bitter, and God forbid that you should learn it through me!'

'But you said you wanted me. Why can't we—?'

'Becky, my grandfather was your grandmother's carpenter. I'm still a carpenter. Sometimes I make a little money repairing cars, getting dirty.'

'Oh, nobody cares about that any more.'

'Ask your father if he cares about it.'

'This has nothing to do with my father. Just you and me.'

Suddenly he lost his temper. 'Don't be stupid!' he shouted.

'Don't call me stupid.'

'You are stupid. If you weren't, you wouldn't come down here and be alone with a man who desires you as much as I do. If you called for help there's nobody to hear you.'

'Why should I need help against you? I know you and—'

'You know nothing,' he said, in a rage. 'I spend my nights lying awake, thinking of you in my bed, in my arms, naked. I have no right to think these things but I can't stop myself. And then you come here, smiling and saying "Luca, I want you", and I go insane. How much do you think one man can take?'

Out of all this only one thing made any impact.

'You desire me?'

'Yes,' he said curtly, turning away to stare out of the window. 'Now go.'

'I'm not going,' she said softly, almost to herself. It was more than a decision. It was a declaration that she had chosen her path and would follow it.

She went close behind him, slipping her arms about his body. As she had known he would, he turned instantly, and fell straight into her trap. She had removed her upper clothing and he found himself holding her bare skin, her arms, her shoulders, her breasts.

He made one last, agonised effort.

'No, Becky—please—'

But the words were drowned by her lips on his, and then it was too late. It had always been too late.

He kissed her tenderly, then with increasing urgency, while his hands explored her and hers explored him. He was wearing a shirt, the front partly unbuttoned. It took her only a moment to rip open the remaining buttons so that she could press her breasts against his body. Inexperienced though she was, she knew at once that the sensation was too much for his self-control. When she moved to pull the shirt right off, he did it for her.

She was completely trusting, without caution or defences, and he seemed to know it even through his passion, for his movements were as controlled as he could make them.

At first all she felt was his tenderness, leading her forward gently. She was already in a fever for him, helping him remove the last of her clothes, then his, following his every move, trying to anticipate, so that he gave a shaky laugh, saying, 'Don't be in such a hurry.'

'But I want you, Luca, *I want you.*'

'But you don't know what you want, *piccina,*' he said hoarsely. 'I have no right—we must stop—'

'*No!* I'll thump you in a minute.'

'Little bully,' he whispered.

'You'd better let me have my own way, then, hadn't you?' she teased.

That was the end of his control. After that, no power on earth could have stopped him exploring her, enchanted by her sweetness and her young, blazing passion for himself.

As soon as he entered her she gave a little cry of excitement and began to move against him, urging him on. Her frank eagerness to make love and her lack of false modesty delighted him, and he gave everything without holding back.

It was a swift, unsubtle mating which came to a climax almost at once. Becky felt dizzy. One moment she was simply enjoying herself, and the next moment something tossed her up to the stars in a fine frenzy of pleasure, before sending her swooping back to earth, wondering which planet she'd landed on. Because it wasn't the same one that she'd started on.

'Oh, wow!' she said breathlessly. 'Oh, wow!'

The next moment she leapt on him again, ignoring his laughing protests. This time he loved her more slowly, or at least as slowly as she would let him, teasing her breasts with lips and fingers, until she wrapped her legs about him, demanding fulfilment, and he could do nothing but yield.

Afterwards they lay entwined while they drifted down from the heights, rejoicing to find each other still there.

'Why did you try to warn me off?' she whispered. 'It was beautiful.'

'I'm glad. I want everything to be beautiful and wonderful for you, always.'

'It *is* wonderful, and you're wonderful, and everything in the world is wonderful, because you love me.'

'I didn't say I loved you,' he growled.

'But you do, don't you?'

'Yes, I do.' He tightened his arms, pulling her naked body hard against his. 'I love you, *piccina*. I love you with my heart and soul, with my body—'

'Yes, I know *that*.' She giggled, letting her fingers run races over his skin.

'Don't tease me,' he groaned. 'I can't endure it.'

'I don't want you to endure it, I want you to give in.'

'Don't I always give in to you?' he asked with a touch of sombreness in his voice.

But that mood couldn't last. She wanted him to make love to her again, and he could never deny her anything.

On the day of Frank's return Becky drove to Pisa Airport to meet him in her own car, delivered as an early birthday gift during his absence.

'I thought you wouldn't want to wait,' he explained now as she thanked him.

'You spoil me, Dad.'

'That's what daughters are for,' he said cheerfully. He was on a 'high' of success, as he told her during the drive home.

'Got everything I wanted at less than I expected to pay. *Yessir!*'

Becky had heard him talk like this many times before, but now the memory of the Englishmen, and their desperation, made it sound different.

'Will anyone be put out of work?' she asked.

'What was that?'

'If you're making such a profit, someone has to lose out, don't they?'

'Of course. Someone always loses out, but they're the wimps, the people who deserve to lose because nature made them losers.'

'But is it nature that makes them losers, or you?'

'Becky, what is this? You've never had such ideas before.'

The thought flashed across her mind, *Or any ideas at all!* But all she said was, 'You closed down a place in England, and some of the people who lost their jobs came out here to find you.'

'The devil they did! What happened?'

'They found me instead. I was out riding alone and three men appeared from nowhere.'

'Did they hurt you?'

'No, but only because a man appeared and saved me. His name's Luca Montese and he lives near by. He was working on his cottage when he heard them shouting. He squared up to them, knocked one of them down and after that they all scurried away.'

'Then I must meet this man and thank him. Where exactly did this happen?'

She described the spot and he frowned.

'I didn't know I had any tenants there.'

'He isn't a tenant, he owns that bit of land. He says you tried to buy him out but he wouldn't sell.'

'Montese?' he muttered. 'Montese? Good grief, that's

him? Carletti, my agent, told me of some fellow who'd been making trouble.'

'He's not making trouble, Dad. He just wants to keep his home.'

'Nonsense, he doesn't know what's good for him. Carletti says the place is little more than a hovel. Squalid, unsanitary.'

'Not any more. He's done a wonderful job of rebuilding it.'

'You've been there?'

'He took me there after he rescued me, and made me some tea. It was nice and cosy. He's worked so hard on it.'

'Well, he's wasting his time. I'll get it in the end.'

'I don't think so. He's determined not to sell.'

'And I'm determined that he will, and I reckon I'm stronger than some peasant lad.'

'Dad!' she cried in protest. 'A moment ago you were going to thank him for saving me. Now you're planning to bully him.'

'Nonsense,' he said with his easy laugh. 'I'll just show him where his best interests lie.'

He visited Luca that same day, full of *bonhomie*, thanking him for his care of Becky while contriving to patronise him in a way that embarrassed her. Luca's response was a quiet dignity.

Then Frank looked around.

'Carletti tells me you've been holding out for more than this little place is worth,' he said.

'Then your agent has misinformed you,' Luca said quietly. 'This place is worth everything to me, and I will not sell.'

'All right, look, here's the deal. Because you helped my daughter I'll double my last offer. I can't say fairer than that.'

'Signor Solway, my home is not for sale.'

'Why make such a fuss about this tatty little place? It's barely half an acre.'

'Then why trouble yourself with it?'

'That doesn't concern you. I've made a more than fair offer and I don't like being trifled with.'

Luca gave his slow smile. It drove Frank Solway mad.

'Have I said something funny?' he snapped.

'*Signor*, I don't think you understand the word no.'

This was so completely right that Frank lost his temper and bawled indiscriminately until Becky said, 'Dad! Have you forgotten what he did for me?'

Frank scowled. He hated to be in the wrong, but neither could he back down. He stomped off without another word, yelling, 'Becky!' over his shoulder.

'Go with him,' Luca said gently when she didn't move.

'No, I'm staying with you.'

'That will make it worse. Please go.'

She yielded to his quiet insistence where her father's blustering only filled her with disgust.

The following day Frank said uneasily, 'I may have gone a little too far with Luca yesterday.'

'Much too far,' Becky said. 'I think you should apologise.'

'No way. That would make me look weak. But you're another matter. Why don't you drop in on him and tell him I'm not such a bad fellow? Don't make it sound like an apology but—well, keep on his right side.'

She left the house with a light heart. Now she could

spend the day with Luca without having to think of an excuse.

He observed her approach from a distance, a quizzical expression on his face.

'Does your father know you're here? Don't get into trouble for me.'

'Are you telling me to go away?' she demanded, hurt.

'It might be better if you did.'

'You sound as if you don't care one way or the other.'

'My back is broad, but yours isn't. I don't want you hurt.'

'In other words you're giving me the brush-off.'

'Don't be stupid,' he growled. 'Of course I don't want you to go.'

She ran into his arms, kissing him again and again.

'I'm not going, my darling. I'm not going to leave you.'

He kissed her long and deeply, and she responded with fierce, young passion. It was he who pulled away first, trembling with the effort it took to rein his desire back, but determined to do so.

'I would die rather than harm you,' he said in a shaking voice.

'But, darling, you're not harming me. Dad told me to come and see you.'

He looked at her wryly. 'And why would he do that?'

She chuckled. 'Can't you guess? He wants me to soften you up for his next offer.'

He grinned. 'And are you going to?'

'Of course not. But he's told me to keep on your right side, and while he thinks that's what I'm doing he won't make a fuss about me coming here. Aren't I clever?'

'You're a cunning little witch.'

'I'm only putting Dad's own theory into practice. He

says when you think someone's acting for you they're always pursuing their own agenda. Well, you're my agenda, so come here and let me get on your right side.'

She took his hand and he went with her, unresisting, because neither then nor later could he deny her anything. It was to be the ruin of both of them.

'Damn you, Luca! You duped me.'

Luca Montese's face showed no relenting. 'Nonsense! You sleepwalked into this without checking.'

'I thought I could trust you.'

'More fool you. I warned you not to trust me, and goodness knows how many of my enemies warned you.'

The man glaring across the desk was in a fury at the thought of the money he'd coveted and lost. His name was—well, no matter. He was the latest in a long line of men who had thought they could put one over on Luca Montese, and found that they were wrong.

'We were supposed to be in this together,' he snapped.

'No. You thought you'd use me as a tool. I was to get the information, then you planned to make a deal behind my back. You should have been more suspicious. When you think a man's acting for you he's always pursuing his own agenda.'

Then a strange thing happened.

As Luca said the words a feeling of malaise came over him, so strong that he had to take a deep breath. It was as though the world had changed in a moment from a place where he was in control to a place where everything was strange and threatening.

'Get out!' he said curtly. 'I'll send you a cheque to cover your expenses.'

The man left fast, relieved simply to recover his expenses, which was more than anyone had got out of Luca for years. He wondered if the monster was losing his touch.

Left alone, Luca held himself still for a long time. The walls seemed to converge on him and suddenly he couldn't breathe.

When you think a man's acting for you he's always pursuing his own agenda.

The words had come so naturally that he'd never doubted they were his own. Yet they had carried a sweetness so unbearable that it had almost destroyed him.

He was choking. He got up and opened the window, but the terrifying memory wouldn't go away.

She had said it, and then she had pulled him down on the bed and loved him until his head was spinning. And he had loved her in return, making her a gift of everything that was in him, heart, body and soul, everything he was or hoped to be.

And that had been his mistake.

It was a mistake he'd never made again in the fifteen years since, when he had piled up money and power. He'd commanded his heart to harden until he could feel nothing, and he had been a success in that, as in everything else.

Now something frightening was happening. More and more the past was calling, tempting him back to a time when he was alive to feeling. But if he worked hard he reckoned he could kill it.

Only one person did not tread carefully when Luca was around, and that was Sonia, his personal assistant. Middle-aged, cool and efficient, she viewed her employer with eyes that were half motherly, half cynical. She was the only person he totally trusted, and with whom he could discuss his personal life.

'Don't waste time brooding,' she advised him over a drink that evening. 'You always said it was a weakness. You've got your divorce, so forget it, and marry again.'

'Never!' he snapped. 'Another barren marriage for people to snicker at? No, thank you.'

'Who says it'll be barren? Just because you didn't have a child by Drusilla doesn't mean a thing. Some couples are like that. They can't have a baby together, but each of them can have a baby by somebody else. Nobody knows why it happens, but it does.

'This hairdresser is her "somebody else". Now you have to find yours. It shouldn't be hard. You're an attractive man.'

He grinned. 'Not like you to pay me compliments. Normally, according to you, I'm an impossible so-and-so with an ego the size of St Peter's dome and—I forget the others but I'm sure you remember them.'

'Selfish, monstrous and intolerable,' she supplied without hesitation. 'I've called you all those things and I don't take back one word.'

'You're probably right.'

'But it doesn't stop you being attractive, and there are millions of women out there.'

He was silent for so long that she wondered if she'd offended him.

'It could work the other way too, couldn't it?' he said at last.

'How do you mean?'

'Suppose there weren't millions of women? Suppose there was only one woman with whom I had any hope of having children?'

'I've never heard of it working that way round.'

'But it might,' he persisted.

'Then you'd have to find her, and it would be like looking for a needle in a haystack.'

'Not if you knew who she was.'

Understanding dawned.

'You've already made your mind up, haven't you? Luca, you don't believe this because it's true, you believe it because you want to. It's rather comforting to know that you can be as irrational as the rest of us.' She regarded him curiously. 'She must have been very special.'

'Yes,' he said heavily. 'She was special.'

He was a man of action. A few phone calls and a representative of the best private-enquiry firm that money could buy was in his office next morning.

'Rebecca Solway,' he said, speaking curtly to hide the fact that his stomach was churning. 'Her father was Frank Solway, owner of the Belleto estate in Tuscany.

'Find her. I don't care what it costs, but *find her*.'

It was a successful evening. Philip Steyne, chairman of the bank, treated Rebecca with honour, and was clearly as impressed as Danvers had hoped he would be. When Rebecca left them for a moment Steyne said,

'Congratulations, Jordan. She'll do the bank credit. When can we expect the announcement?'

'Any day, I hope. Nothing's been said precisely, but of course she understands where we're heading.'

'Well, in good banking it pays to be precise,' observed Steyne with a grin. 'Don't take too long.'

When Rebecca returned he said, 'Rebecca, let me have the benefit of your expertise. You're a quarter Italian, right?'

'Yes, my father's mother came from Tuscany.'

'And you speak the language?'

She gave him her cleverest smile, a little bit teasing, but not too much. This was Danvers' boss.

'Which language do you mean? There's *la madre lingua*, the official language that they use on radio and television, and in government. But there are also the regional dialects, which are languages in themselves. I speak *la madre lingua*, and Tuscan.'

'I'm impressed. Actually Tuscan might be handy. This firm has its head office in Rome, but I believe it started in Tuscany, and it's all over the world now.'

'Firm?'

'Raditore Inc. Property, finance, finger in every pie. Suddenly it's buying a huge block of shares in the Allingham, and the bank's interested in closer contact. I propose a dinner party at my house—you, Danvers, their top brass. Let's see what there is to be gained from them.'

Driving her home, Danvers was lyrical in his praise.

'You really impressed the old man tonight, darling.'

'Good. I'm glad I was a help to you.'

She answered mechanically and he shot her a quick sideways look, thinking that this was the second time she'd been in a funny mood and he hoped it wasn't going to become a habit.

Again she didn't invite him into her suite, which he found annoying. He would have found it convenient to discuss the forthcoming dinner party. Instead Rebecca bid him an implacable goodnight and shut her door.

When he was out of sight she closed her eyes in relief, then stripped off hurriedly and got under the shower, wanting to wash the evening away. She was on edge tonight, just as she had been the night before. The mention of Tuscany had unsettled her, and the ghost had walked again.

CHAPTER THREE

As soon as Becky was certain, she hurried to tell Luca the news. He was thrilled.

'A baby? Our own little *bambino*! Half you, half me.'

'Your very own son and heir,' she said, snuggling blissfully in his arms.

How he laughed.

'I'm just a common labourer. Labourers don't have heirs. Besides, I want a girl—just like you. I want another Becky.'

Her pregnancy brought out the best in him, and she discovered again that he was a marvellous man, loving, tender, considerate as few men knew how to be. Later, when joy was replaced by anguish, it was his tenderness that Rebecca remembered most wistfully. How gently he took care of her, how worried he always was about her health. Nothing was ever too much trouble for him to do for her.

Her father was away a lot that summer, visiting his various interests, and there was little chance to tell him. When he did return it was only for a few days, filled with phone calls. Becky didn't want to break the news until she was sure of having all his attention, so she waited until she knew he would be home for at least two weeks. By that time she was three months gone.

'And you will tell him this time?' Luca asked.

'Of course. I only want everything to be right when I do.'

'I want to be with you. I won't have you face his anger alone.'

'What anger? Dad will be thrilled,' she predicted blithely. 'He loves babies.'

It was true. Like many bullies Frank Solway had a streak of sentimentality. He cooed over babies and the world said what a delightful man he was.

'Honestly, darling,' Becky said, 'this will make everything all right.'

How stupid could you be?

Her father was almost out of his mind with rage.

'You got yourself knocked up by that...?' He finished on a stream of profanity.

'Dad, I didn't get "knocked up". I got pregnant by a man I love. Please don't try to make it sound like something dirty.'

'It is dirty. How dare he lay a finger on you?'

'Because I wanted him to. To put it plainly, *I* dragged *him* into bed, not the other way around.'

'Don't ever let me hear you say that again,' he shouted.

'It's true! I love Luca and I'm going to marry him.'

'You think I'm going to allow that? You think my daughter is going to marry that low-life? The sooner this is fixed the better.'

'I'm going to have my baby.'

'The hell you are!'

She ran away that night. Frank followed her to Luca's house and tried to buy her back. But the mention of money only made Luca roar with laughter. Later Becky was to realise what her father heard in that laughter. It was the roar of the young lion telling the old lion that

he no longer ruled. Perhaps her father's real hatred dated
from that moment.

He tried to enlist the help of the locals, but he was
thwarted. Frank Solway was powerful but Luca was one
of them, and nobody was ready to raise their hand
against him.

But Becky knew he wouldn't give up, and in the end
it was she who suggested they leave.

'Just for a while, darling. Dad'll feel better about it
when he's a grandfather.'

He sighed. 'I hate running away, but all this quarrel-
ling is bad for you and the baby. We'll go for the sake
of some peace.'

They fled south to stay with his friends in Naples.
After two weeks he bought an old car, repaired it him-
self, and they set off again, heading south to Calabria.
Two weeks there, then north again.

They talked about marriage but never stayed anywhere long enough to complete the formalities, just in
case Frank's tentacles reached them. Wherever they
went his skilled hands found him work. It was a good
life.

Becky had not known that such happiness was possible. She was over the first sickness of pregnancy, feeling well and strong, spending her life with the man she
adored. Their love was the unquestioning, uncompli-
cated kind that inspired songs and stories, with a happy-
ever-after always promised at the end. She loved him,
he loved her, and their baby would arrive soon. What
more was there?

The thought of Frank was always there in the back-
ground, but as week followed week with no sign of him

he faded and became unreal, a 'maybe' rather than a genuine threat.

She began to understand Luca better, and herself. It was Luca who revealed her body to her, its fierce responses, its eagerness for physical love. But it was also through him, and the life they lived, that she was able to stand outside herself, and look with critical eyes. What she saw did not please her.

'I was horrid,' she said to him once. 'A real spoilt brat, taking everything for granted, letting Dad indulge me and never wondering where the money came from. But it actually came from men like the ones who stopped me that day. He practically stole from them. You can't really blame them, can you?'

'You can't blame yourself, either,' he insisted. 'You were so young, how could it occur to you to ask questions about your father's methods? But when your eyes were opened you didn't try to look away. My Becky is too brave for that.'

There was always a special note in his voice when he said 'my Becky', as though all the best in her was a personal gift to himself, to be treasured. It made her feel like the most important person in the world. And in the world they made together, that was true.

She gradually came to understand that Luca was one person to her, and a different man to everyone else. The attackers who had fled him, filled with fear, had seen the side of him that others saw.

He was a potentially frightening man who carried with him an aura of being always on the edge of ruthlessness, even violence. It took time for Becky to understand this, because he never showed that side of himself to her.

They had their arguments, even outright rows, but he

fought fair, never turning his ferocity on her, and always bringing the spat to a speedy end, often by simply giving in. It hurt him to be at odds with her.

In their daily life he was tender, loving and gentle, setting her on a pedestal and asserting, by his actions, that she was different from all other human beings on earth.

His love for her carried a hint of worship that awed and delighted her, even while it sometimes made him over-protective to the point of being dictatorial. It was he who decided, in her sixth month, that their lovemaking must cease until after the baby was born, and she had fully recovered.

Torn by desire, she wept and pleaded. 'It's too soon. The doctor says we've time yet.'

'The doctor is not the father of your baby. *I am*, and *I* have decided that it is time to stop,' he declared in the most arrogant statement she had yet heard from him.

'But what will you do? It's months and months, and you'll—well, you know.'

'What are you saying? That you don't trust me to be faithful to you?'

'Well, I don't know, do I?' she cried.

There was a flash of temper on his face, for he had never given her a moment's cause for anxiety. But anger was gone in a instant, dissolved in laughter.

'Oh, stop that,' she said, thumping him in frustration.

But he roared aloud with laughter, holding her carefully against him.

'*Amor mia,* I promise to be home at the proper time every evening, and you may put a collar and lead about my neck,' he said with a grin.

'And every man in the place will say you're living under my thumb, and laugh at you.'

'But I don't care what they think, only what you think,' he said, serious again. 'You and our child are everything in life to me.'

He stuck to his resolve, keeping an iron control over himself, and spending all his spare time at home. Becky, talking to other expectant mothers in doctors' waiting rooms, knew just how lucky she was.

For most of the time she could push serious matters aside to enjoy their life. Everything was fun. Being poor, learning how to shop so that she got the best out of his wages, living in old jeans and letting them out as she put on weight—all this was fun.

It was Luca who finally decided that they should settle in one spot. She was now more than six months gone, and he said, 'I want you under the care of the same doctor from now on.'

They had reached Carenna, a small town near Florence, where he had found work with a local builder. It was a pleasant place to put down roots. He located a good doctor, found some birth classes, and attended them with her, mastering all the exercises, to her tender amusement. At home they practised together until they collapsed with laughter.

Perhaps so much happiness could never last. Sometimes it seemed as though she'd used up her lifetime's allowance in those few glorious months.

Philip Steyne's house was on the edge of London. As befitted his money, it was a mansion, set in its own grounds, with far more rooms than he needed.

The dinner party was for twenty, a number just large

enough to allow a mix, but small enough for the right people to home in on each other.

Rebecca knew what was expected of her and dressed accordingly in a dress of wine-red velvet that hugged her slender figure. Black silk stockings sheathed her legs, finishing in dainty black sandals. Tonight she let her long blonde hair flow freely in a 'natural' style that had taken the beauty parlour three hours to perfect, and which set the seal on her glamour. Her solid gold necklace and earrings were Danvers' gift 'to mark the occasion'.

'We still don't know who's actually coming tonight,' he remarked as the car purred into the drive. 'Raditore has played coy as to whether it'll be the chairman, chief executive or managing director.'

'Does it matter?' she asked. 'I know my job, and I it'll be much the same whoever it is.'

'That's right. Just make his head spin. I must say, you're dressed for it. I've never seen you looking so good.'

'Thank you.'

'I'm always proud of you.'

'Thank you,' she said again, speaking mechanically. It was hard to respond in any way, since Danvers paid compliments as though ticking off a list.

The car glided silently through the gate, down the long drive to the house. When they were nearly there Rebecca had a moment of strange and disturbing consciousness.

Suddenly the luxurious car was every luxurious car she had ever journeyed in, the huge, moneyed house was the end of a long line of moneyed houses, the dinner

party to meet rich men, and charm them, was indistinguishable from so many—too many—others.

There was the house, the front door being pulled open,
her hosts coming out onto the step, welcoming smiles in
place. Philip Steyne's suit had been tailored in Savile
Row, his wife's dress was haute couture. Like so many
others.

'Danvers, Rebecca, how *lovely* to see you. Come in,
come—Rebecca, you look *lovely* as always—what a
lovely dress...'

The same words said a hundred times by a hundred
people. And her own response, indistinguishable from
before. The same smiles, the same laughter, the same
emptiness.

Philip Steyne murmured in her ear, 'Well done. You'll
reduce him to jelly.'

'Is he here?'

'Arrived ten minutes ago. Just through here.'

Again, just as before. But then, thankfully, the moment passed and she was free again to live her life on
the surface, without thinking or feeling too much.
Because only in that way was existence tolerable.

It had been a bad few minutes, but she was all right
again now.

It was in this mood that she walked into the next room
and saw Luca Montese for the first time in fifteen years.

Now they were settled they could plan the wedding.

'*Carissima,* you don't mind a simple ceremony with
no gorgeous bridal gown?'

She chuckled. 'I'd look a bit odd in a gorgeous bridal
gown and a seven-month bulge. And I don't want fuss.
I just want you.'

They were going to bed and he tucked her up, then knelt down beside her, taking her hands in his and speaking in a low, reverent voice that she had never heard before.

'The day after tomorrow we will be married. We shall stand before God and make sacred promises. But I tell you that none of them will be as sacred as those I make to you now. I promise you that my heart, my love and my whole life belong to you, and always will.'

He spoke like a man uttering a prayer.

'Do you understand?' he urged. 'Whether my life be long or short, every moment of it will be spent in your service.'

He laid his hand gently over her bulge.

'And you, little one—you too I will love and protect in every way. You will be safe and happy, because your *mama* and *papa* love you.'

Becky tried to answer him, but no words would come through her tears.

'Oh, Luca,' she managed to say at last, 'if I could only tell you—'

'Hush, *carissima*. You do not need to tell me what I see in your eyes.'

He took her face between his hands and looked down at her searchingly.

'You will always be to me as you are at this moment,' he whispered before kissing her with heart-stopping gentleness.

She slept in his arms that night, and awoke to his kiss in the early morning. He was going to work sooner than usual, so that he could come home early to help with last-minute preparations for their wedding.

Becky spent the day tidying the house, and making

sure they had enough food and wine for their friends. She was just putting the kettle on for a much needed cup of tea when the doorbell rang.

It was almost a relief to find Frank standing there. She felt safer now, because surely her bulge would make him accept the inevitable?

'Hello, Dad.'

'Hello, Becky. Can I come in?'

He entered without seeming to notice her shape. He had a gift for not noticing what didn't suit him.

'You're on your own, I see. Got tired of you already, has he?'

'Dad, it's three in the afternoon. He's at work, but he'll be home any minute.'

'So you say.'

She'd known then that it wasn't going to be easy after all. But she tried.

'It's nice to see you—'

'Yes, I expect you're fed up with all this.'

'No, I'm not. This is my life. Look around you at all this food and wine. It's for our wedding reception to-morrow.'

He shot her a sharp look.

'So you're not married? Good, then I'm in time.'

'I'm having Luca's baby, and I'm going to marry him,' she said firmly. 'Won't you come to the wedding and drink our health, and be our friend?'

He looked down at her with an expression that might have been tenderness.

'Darling, you're living in a dream world. Trust me, I know what's best for you. He's deluded you.'

'Dad—'

'But I'm here to make it right. Just let me take care of you. Everything will be fine as soon as we're home.'

'This *is* my home.'

'This—this hovel? You think I'm leaving you here? Stop arguing *and come on.*'

Abruptly he dropped the pretence of kindness, and seized her arm. She shrieked. Luca, approaching the house, heard her and rushed the rest of the way, flinging open the door to find them struggling.

'Let her go,' he roared.

'Get out of my way,' Frank snapped.

Luca stood there, barring the door. 'I said let her go.'

Frank ignored him, trying to drag her towards the back door by sheer force. Becky struggled as hard as she could, but her size made it difficult.

With a curse Luca strode forward and placed one powerful hand on Frank's arm.

'Don't dare touch her,' he said, and there was the same menace in his eyes that she had seen before, when they had first met.

'I'm taking her home,' Frank repeated.

Luca's voice was infused with contempt.

'You are not only a bully but a deeply stupid man. Only a *cretino* would do this, knowing that he was threatening the well-being of the child she carries.'

Frank's answer was to try again to drag Becky away. Luca did not move, but his hand, grasping the other man's arm, was impossible to dislodge.

'Luca, don't let him take me,' she begged.

That sent Frank over the edge, and he began to rant and rave. Luca said nothing, merely standing silent and immovable. Perhaps it was that quiet dignity that infuriated Frank most, for he shoved Becky aside to contend with Luca.

Then the nightmare started. Heaving with distress, Becky suddenly found the world retreating and returning alarmingly. Everything seemed to spin around, culminating in a feeling of knives searing through her.

She screamed and doubled over as agony engulfed her like a furnace. The sound got through to the two men, halting their fight, although even then Frank had to put himself centre stage. Her last clear sight was of him shouldering his way ahead of Luca to lean over her.

But it was Luca she wanted. She reached out, calling his name, but Frank was there, leaning close, grasping her tightly, imprisoning her, blocking out everything but himself.

'Luca,' she screamed. *'Luca!'*

But suddenly he vanished. She never saw him again.

An ambulance came to whisk her off to hospital. Her daughter was born quickly and died within a few hours.

When the physical pain ceased there was another pain waiting, in her mind. Fire turned to ice as a merciless darkness enclosed her. The only thing she knew for sure was that she called repeatedly for Luca, but he was never there.

How could he not be there? His daughter had been born, and had died without his ever holding her in his arms. He had promised to love and protect her, but he hadn't been there when she needed him.

'She was so little and helpless,' she whispered into the void. 'She needed her father.'

But he did not hear. The darkness had swallowed him up.

Scenes changed about her. Somehow she knew that

she was back in England, and living in a new place, a large, pleasant house where there were people in white coats and everyone spoke in kindly voices.

Sometimes the voices were brisk and hearty. 'How are we feeling today? A little better? That's good.'

She never answered, but they didn't seem to mind. They treated her like a doll, brushing her hair and talking about her as though she wasn't there.

'There's no way of knowing how long she'll be like this, Mr Solway. She has profound post-natal depression, aggravated by terrible inner wounds, and they need time to heal.'

She never reminded them that she was a living being with thoughts and feelings, because she no longer felt like one. It was easier this way because they didn't expect her to respond, and the soul-deep exhaustion that possessed her made answering seem like climbing a mountain.

Often the words she heard were a meaningless jabber, but one day the world righted itself and she began to hear and see it normally. Frank was in the middle of one of his monologues, and the words made sense.

'...Not easy coming back to England—wrong time of the financial year—left me with a hefty tax bill, but I said only the best was good enough for my girl. And this place *is* the best. Oh, yes, no skimping.'

'Where is he? Where's Luca? Why doesn't he come to see me?'

'Because he's gone, for good. I bought him off.'

She turned her head slowly and stared at him with a look that made even that thick-skinned man flinch.

'What do you mean?' Even to her own ears her voice sounded dead and metallic.

'I mean I bought him off. He demanded money to go away and never trouble you again.'

'I—don't—believe—you.' The words came out like hammer taps.

'Then I'll prove it.'

His proof was a cheque for the euro equivalent of fifty thousand pounds, made out to Luca Montese, with the record, on the back, of the bank where it had been cashed.

She wanted to say that it was false, it proved nothing. But she knew the bank Luca used in Tuscany, and it was the same one.

Whether my life be long or short, every moment of it will be spent in your service.

How long after saying those words had he sold her back to her father for cash?

She had thought she was dead already, but there must still have been some feeling left alive, because she sensed the last remnants die at that moment. And was glad of it.

Everyone agreed that the meal was superb. The wine was a hundred-year-old vintage and the brandy even older.

Luca Montese had been the centre of attention from the start. As the guests entered, one by one, they were introduced to him—presented to him, Rebecca thought—in a way that left no doubt he was the guest of honour. But even without that he would have held attention by the magnetism that seemed to surround him like a force field.

His eyes were like flint. His smile was wolfish. He was a predator, coolly surveying the prey around him, counting them off in order of their importance to him.

They all knew it, of course they did. And each of them was courting him.

Except herself.

'Luca,' Philip Steyne said jovially, 'let me introduce you to one of my favourite people, Rebecca Hanley, who takes care of PR for the Allingham.'

'Then Mrs Hanley is a most important person to me,' Luca responded at once.

'Good evening, Signor Montese,' Rebecca replied coolly.

He felt different. The hand that engulfed hers was no longer the rough paw that had held her in passion and tenderness, and which she had loved. It was smooth and manicured, a rich man's hand. A stranger's.

She forced herself to meet his eyes, and found nothing there. No warmth, no alarm, no amazement, no recognition. Nothing.

Relief and disappointment warred, but neither won.

She disengaged her hand at once and murmured something about the pleasure of meeting him. There were people behind her, agog for an introduction, and they provided an excuse for her not to linger.

'You might have been a bit more gracious,' Danvers complained under his breath when he too had been introduced and passed on. 'These self-made men can be so touchy if they think they're being patronised.'

'But you're the one who's patronising him,' she pointed out.

'What?'

'The way you said ''these self-made men'' was deeply patronising. As though they're all alike.'

'They are, more or less. Full of themselves. Always wanting to tell you how they did it.'

Rebecca maintained a diplomatic silence. It would have been ill-natured to point out that Danvers had been born to money and therefore had nothing to tell.

She was getting her second wind. There had been the shock of meeting him without warning, but that was over now, and she could study him while he talked with somebody else.

She would hardly have known him. His height and breadth of shoulder were the same, but his hair, which had always been shaggy, tempting her to run her fingers through it, was cut back neat and short, revealing the lines of his face. The large nose with the hint of a hook was the one she knew, but the rest was strange.

'A rough diamond,' Philip Steyne murmured in her ear. 'But very rich. And when you think that he came from nowhere, and started with nothing!'

'Nobody really starts with nothing,' Danvers observed. 'Somehow, somewhere he got his hands on a lump sum of money to begin with. One can only speculate on what he had to do to get it.'

'Perhaps he'll tell you,' Rebecca said sharply. 'That's what "self-made men" do, isn't it?'

Danvers shared a grin with Steyne. 'Maybe it's best if we don't know,' he observed. 'He looks as though he could be an ugly customer.'

Rebecca said no more. She knew what Luca had done to get his start.

She had last seen him penniless. Now he was so rich and powerful that one of the biggest merchant banks in the country put itself out for him.

That alone revealed part of the story. She had mixed with financiers long enough to know the kind of men who prospered in that atmosphere. Luca's success told her that he had become everything he had once despised.

What his prosperity didn't tell her, his face did. The open, generous candour that had made him lovable was gone. In its place was hardness, even ruthlessness, eyes that glinted with suspicion where once they had shone with joy. An ugly customer.

Her father had said, 'He demanded money to go away and never trouble you again.'

Even after seeing the cheque she had sometimes repeated to herself that it couldn't be true. If he had returned she would gladly have believed any explanation. But she never heard from him again, and at last she had stopped crying the words into the darkness.

Seeing him now, she knew that the worst was true. Luca had needed money, and he had sold their love to get it.

As they entered the dining room she braced herself, knowing that she would be sitting next to him.

The bait in the trap, she thought wearily. Oh, what does it matter?

He did everything correctly, like a man used to dining amid wealth. After making a few brief, meaningless observations to her, he paid courteous attention to the lady on his other side, who was his hostess.

So far, so good. Nothing to alarm her.

Then Philip Steyne said jovially, 'Luca, in case you're wondering why we sat you next to Rebecca, it's because she speaks Italian, even Tuscan.'

'That was very kind of you,' Luca said. 'So, *signora*,' he turned his attention to Rebecca and slipped into Tuscan to say, 'are we going to go all evening pretending not to know each other?'

CHAPTER FOUR

So HE had known all the time, and picked his own moment to reveal it. Taken by surprise, Rebecca couldn't control a swift gasp.

The others were watching them, smiling, enjoying what they thought of as the joke.

'What did he say, Rebecca?' Philip asked. 'It must have been quite something to make you gasp like that. Come on, tell.'

'Oh, no,' she said brightly. 'I know how to keep a secret.'

Everyone laughed as if she'd made a brilliant witticism. Still smiling, she met Luca's eyes.

'Do we know each other?' she asked, also in Tuscan.

'Yes,' he said flatly. 'Why pretend?'

'Have you told anyone else?'

'No. That wouldn't suit me. Or you, I imagine.'

He was right, but it was intolerable that he took her reaction for granted.

'No,' she said briefly.

'No problem, then.'

'You're a remarkably cool customer.'

'Not now.'

'What did you say?'

'We can't discuss it now. There are too many people about. We'll talk later.'

His assumption that the decision was only his infuriated her.

'We will not talk later,' she said in a low voice. 'I shall be leaving early.'

He gave her an unexpected grin.

'No, you won't,' he said.

'Are you trying to give me orders?'

'No, just saying that you don't really mean it.'

'You're damned sure of yourself,' she said.

'Am I?' He seemed surprised. 'I couldn't go away without talking to you. Not after all this time. I just thought maybe you couldn't, either. Am I wrong?'

'No,' she said, annoyed with herself because it was true.

Luca addressed the rest of the table with an expansive smile.

'I can't fault this lady. Her Tuscan is perfect.'

Everyone applauded. Rebecca saw Danvers and Philip exchange triumphant glances.

She got through the rest of the meal somehow. When it came to the coffee everyone left the table and went into the huge conservatory. The double doors were wide open and many people drifted into the beautiful grounds, where the trees were hung with coloured lights.

'Come outside and show me the grounds,' Luca said.

Wanting to get this meeting over with, she followed him out and along the path that the lights dimly outlined. As they went she talked of trees and shrubs, pointing out the features of the landscaped garden in a voice that gave nothing away.

But at last he paused under the trees and said in Tuscan, 'We can drop the polite nothings now.'

'I really should be going back—'

'Not yet.' He put out a hand to restrain her, but she

withdrew before he could make contact, and he let his hand drop.

'Did you think we would ever meet again?' he asked.

'No,' she said softly. 'Never.'

'Of course. How could we ever meet again in the world? Everything was against it.'

'Everything was always against us,' she said. 'We never really stood a chance.'

He took a step closer and looked at her face in the light from the moon and a pink lamp hanging above them.

'You've changed,' he said. 'And yet you haven't. Not really.'

'You've changed in every way,' she said.

He rubbed the scar awkwardly. 'You mean this?'

'No, I mean everything about you.'

'I'm fifteen years older. A good deal has happened to me. And to you.'

'Yes.' She was being deliberately monosyllabic, refusing to give anything away. In some mysterious way he alarmed her now, as he had never done before.

'Your name has changed,' he said, 'so you've been married. But the man with you isn't called Hanley.'

'Yes, I'm divorced from Saul Hanley.'

'Were you married long?'

'Six years.'

'Did your father approve of him?'

'He was dead by the time I married. I didn't see him much in the last years of his life. We had nothing to say. He couldn't look me in the eye.'

'No wonder.'

The words brought them to the edge of dangerous ground, and she shied away.

'And you?' she asked lightly. 'I'm sure you have a wife at home.'

'Why should you be sure?'

'Because every successful man needs a wife to host his dinner parties.'

'I don't give dinner parties. Drusilla used to enjoy them, so we had a few, but we're divorced now.'

'Because she wanted dinner parties?' she asked, trying to make a joke of it.

'No,' he said abruptly. 'Other reasons.'

'I'm sorry, I didn't mean to pry.'

'No problem. Tell me what else you've been doing.'

The words sounded abrupt, ungracious, but she doubted if he had meant them that way. She guessed that Luca Montese's social skills were only skin deep.

'I sold the estate and went travelling. When I came home I did some book translating, using my Italian. That was how I met Saul. He was a publisher.'

'Why did you divorce him?'

'It was a mutual decision,' she said after a moment. 'We weren't suited.'

They had been strolling around the paths, and now the house was in view again.

'Perhaps we should go inside,' she said.

'I have something to say first.'

'Yes?'

He seemed to be having difficulty, then he blurted out, 'I want to see you again. Alone.'

'No, Luca,' she said quickly. 'There's no point.'

'That doesn't make any sense. Of course there's a point. I want to talk to you. It all happened too abruptly. We never even had the chance to say goodbye. We've each spent years not knowing what happened to the other, and there's a lot I want to explain. I'm entitled to the chance.'

'Don't talk to me like that,' she said, offended.

'Like what?' He was genuinely puzzled.

'Making demands, talking about what you're entitled to. You're not addressing a board meeting.'

'I just want you to understand.'

Did he think any explanation would make things better? she wondered.

'Luca, if it's about the money, you don't have to say anything. I'm sure it was all for the best in the long run. I should congratulate you. You must have used it very shrewdly.'

A strange look came over his face. 'Ah, your father told you about the money? I wondered.'

'Of course he did,' she said, feeling a pang of pain that he could speak about it so casually. 'So we can draw a line under it.'

'And that's all you have to say? Good God, Becky, have you no questions to ask me after all this time?'

'The girl I was then had questions, and the boy you were might have answered them.'

'He'd have tried. He always tried to do what you wanted, because he had no pleasure but your happiness. Have you forgotten that?'

She hadn't forgotten it but she had put it away in darkness, hoping never to think of it again.

'No,' she said at last. 'I hadn't forgotten. But it's too late now. We're not those people any more. We last saw each other fifteen years ago, the day before our wedding, when my father burst in. And I'm really glad you've made a success of your life—'

He stared at her. 'What was that you said?'

'I'm glad you've been successful—'

'No, before that, about our last meeting.'

'It was on the day before our wedding—or what should have been our wedding.'

'Then you don't remember...?' He checked himself. 'Well, perhaps it's not surprising. But it's even more important to see each other again. We have unfinished business, and it's time to take care of it.'

She gave a little shudder. She wanted nothing to do with this man who had Luca's name and a face that resembled his but had nothing else of him. Luca had been tender and gentle. This stranger barked his orders even when he was trying to make human contact. If this was what Luca had turned into, she wished she had never known.

'I'm sorry,' she said, trying to speak calmly. 'But I can see no point in a further meeting.'

'But I can,' he said bluntly.

She took a deep breath, trying to keep her temper.

'Unfortunately both sides need to be willing, and I'm not.'

'*They* won't be pleased if you snub me,' he said, jerking his head towards the house.

So he knew that she'd been told to charm him. Of course he did.

'*They* can conduct their business without my help,' she retorted crisply, and began to walk away from him.

'Are you going to marry Danvers Jordan?' he called after her.

She turned and asked, 'What did you say?' in a tone that was meant to warn him.

'I want to know.'

'But it does not suit me to tell you,' she said slowly and emphatically. 'Goodnight, Signor Montese.'

She hoped she could slip back into the conservatory without attracting attention, in case someone should wonder why she was alone. But Luca caught up and entered behind her, just close enough to make it look as if they were still together. To her relief he did not try to talk to her again for the rest of the evening.

But when they said goodbye he held her hand a little too long and said softly, *'Arrivederci per ora.'* Goodbye for now.

And she answered swiftly, *'Mai piu.'* Never more.

She would not see him again, and it was best that he knew it now.

He said nothing but released her hand and turned away.

On the way home Danvers said, 'Well done, darling, you made a hit with Montese. He couldn't speak highly enough of you.'

'I wish I could say the same,' she said, sounding bored. 'I thought he was an impossible man. Rude, vulgar, graceless—'

'Oh, of course. What can you expect? But as a money man he's got no equal.'

'I just hope I don't have to see him again.'

'I'm afraid you will. Apparently he's going to be living at the Allingham.'

'But why?' she cried in protest before she could stop herself.

'He has no home in this country. It makes sense for him to live in a hotel, and naturally he picks the one where he owns stock. It's perfectly reasonable.'

Of course it was reasonable. It was so reasonable that it alarmed her.

'When did he tell you this?'

'Just before we left. That's why I say you did a brilliant job. And Steyne is bowled over by you. He keeps dropping hints about my "acquiring a prize asset".'

The right response would turn this into a proposal, one that had been long expected. She took a deep breath and said, 'That's nice of him.' She yawned. 'Oh, dear, I hadn't realised I was so tired. Just drop me at the door, and I'll go straight up to bed.'

He accepted his dismissal without complaint, although his goodbye was rather chilly. She couldn't help it. When they reached the Allingham she said goodnight and walked quickly away.

Nigel Haleworth, the hotel's managing director, was a genially cynical man. Rebecca got on well with him, and at their regular weekly meeting next morning, when routine business had been dealt with, he said with a grin, 'You've met King Midas, I gather. He's arriving today. Penthouse suite, of course.'

'King Midas?'

'Luca Montese. Do you remember the story of Midas?'

'Yes. He made a wish that everything around him should turn to gold,' she remembered. 'But he forgot his beloved daughter, and when he touched her she too turned to gold. He was left with nobody to love.'

'Right. That's what they say about Montese—not the daughter bit, because he has no children. But there's nothing in his life but money.'

'I believe he's divorced.'

'A few months ago. Touchy subject. A "king" likes to have an heir, but he never managed to make her pregnant in six years of marriage. Then she had a baby by another man.

'You can imagine what that did to him. I gather he's a very frightening man if you're on his wrong side. He's made a thousand enemies, and they're all jeering at him behind their hands—what's wrong with "the king" that he can't do what any other man can do? That sort of thing.'

'It's nonsense,' said Rebecca sharply. 'They may just have been incompatible.'

'Or maybe he simply can't father a child. That's what they're whispering.'

Rebecca shrugged. 'If they're his enemies they'll believe what they like.'

'What did you think of him?'

After a moment she said, 'Let's say that I can understand why he has enemies.'

'Why not research him a bit before he arrives?'

Back in her suite she logged on to the internet.

English websites carried little about Luca or his firm, but Italian ones were more informative. Raditore had swiftly risen from a small outfit to a huge conglomerate with a speed that spoke volumes of its owner's skill and lack of scruple. But there was nothing about his personal life. He might never have had one.

And that was it, she realised suddenly. The man she had met the previous evening had seemed to have no hinterland beyond his fixation on herself, as though he'd shut down every part of himself except one.

Now she could feel something for him, and it was

pity. She had frozen to protect herself from insupport-able pain. Had he done the same?

She found a multitude of urgent tasks to prevent her from being in the hotel when Luca arrived that after-noon. When she returned she was in a more settled frame of mind, even willing to concede that they needed to talk.

Doubtless he would call her and they would meet for a sedate dinner. They would bring each other up to date, after which she would be freed from ghosts. Feeling calm and prepared, she waited for the phone to ring.

Instead there was a knock on the door. Frowning, she opened it.

'This is for you, ma'am,' said the man with the pack-age. 'Please sign here.'

When he had gone she opened the package cautiously, and found a jewel case.

Inside lay the most fabulous set of diamonds that she had ever seen. A necklace of three strands, earrings, bracelet, brooch. All of the very best. Rebecca's expe-rienced eye told her that there was nearly a hundred thousand pounds' worth of jewels here.

The small card bore only the two words. *Per adesso.* For now.

She sat down, alarmed to find that she was trembling.

For now? It was almost a threat, implying that he would not accept her dismissal.

Why couldn't he leave her to her hard-won peace? Didn't he want peace himself?

At last she pulled herself together and headed out of the door. It took her five minutes to reach the penthouse suite, and her anger rose with every step.

'How dare you?' she said when he opened the door.

'Please take this back, and don't ever do such a thing again.'

He backed away from her, forcing her to come into the room to find somewhere to set the case down.

'I mean what I say. I don't want these things. Luca, what were you thinking of? You can't send something like this to a stranger.'

'You're not a stranger. You can't be.'

'I must be after all these years. Too much has happened. We're different people. I don't accept this kind of gift.'

'You mean not from me, because I'm not good enough?'

'Don't be absurd. Of course you're good enough. How can you say such a thing to me, after our past?' She lost her temper. 'I think I've earned better than that from you.'

'All right, I'm sorry,' he said gruffly. 'Maybe I'm not so different from what I was. Maybe, inside, I'm still the bumpkin your father looked down on. I can change the outside but not in here.' He pointed to himself. 'I hear the sneers, even when they're whispered.'

'But I never sneered at you.'

'So what's wrong with me giving you something?'

'This isn't "something", it's a fortune.'

'Do you take diamonds from him?' he demanded abruptly.

'Luca, stop that. I'm not answerable to you.'

He scowled, and she wondered how long it had been since anyone stood up to him, and said no. A long time, she suspected, since he didn't know how to cope with it.

'It's a simple question,' he grated.

'And I'll give you a simple answer. Mind your own damned business. Who do you think you are to turn up in my life after fifteen years and take anything for granted?'

'All right.' He threw up his hands. 'I've managed it badly. Let's start again.'

'No, let's just leave it here. We met again and found that we're strangers. There was no lightning flash. The past doesn't live again and it certainly can't be put right. Love dies, and once dead it can't be revived.'

'Love?' he snapped. 'Have I asked for your love? You flatter yourself.'

'Well, you certainly wanted something in return for diamonds. And I don't flatter myself, because it doesn't flatter me to be pursued by a man who approaches a woman as though he were buying stocks and shares. I am not a piece of property.'

'Aren't you? Well, it sure as hell looked like it last night.'

'What do you mean by that?'

'They paraded you in front of me, didn't they? First you sat next to me, then you led me out into the garden. Did you think I didn't know what was going on? Sweet-talk him! That's what they told you. Make his head spin so that we can milk him of his money. Wasn't it something like that?'

She faced him defiantly. 'It was exactly like that. What else would make me go out into the garden with you?'

It was cruel, but she was desperate to make him back off. He threatened the stability it had cost her too much to achieve.

But she was sorry when she saw the colour drain from

his face, leaving it a deathly grey. She had meant only to stab at his pride, as a warning. She might have thought he was hurt to the heart, if she believed that he still had a heart.

'Look, I'm sorry,' she said. 'That was cheap and unjust. I didn't mean to hurt you—'

'You can't,' he said curtly. 'Don't worry yourself.'

There was a knock on the door, and a faint call of, 'Room Service.'

Luca made a sign that he would be back and went to the door. Left alone, Rebecca looked around for somewhere to leave the diamonds so that there would be no more arguing about them.

The door to the bedroom was open and she could see the small chest of drawers against the bed, with a heavy lamp on top. Luca was still at the front door, and she had time to slip into the bedroom and pull open the top drawer, ready to thrust the box inside.

She had to move some papers aside to make room for it. Some were in a large open envelope that spilled its contents as it was moved. What Rebecca saw made her stop dead.

A photograph had fallen out. It showed a young girl with windblown hair and a young, eager face. She was sitting on the top rail of a fence, laughing at the cameraman, her eyes full of love and joy.

Luca had taken it on the day she told him about the baby. Even if she had not remembered, she would have known that from the look on her own face. This was a girl who had everything, and was sure she could never lose it.

And Luca had kept this picture with him.

It was as though someone had given him back to her.

Suddenly her anger at him melted and she wanted to find him and share the moment.

'Luca...'

She turned eagerly and saw him standing, watching her, his face defenceless, possessed by a look that mirrored her own feelings. He was there again, the boy she had loved, and who still lived somewhere in this harsh, aggressive man.

'Luca,' she said again.

And then it was gone. The light in his eyes shut down, the mask was back in place.

'What are you doing in here?' he snapped.

'I wasn't prying—'

'Then why are you here?'

She realised that he was really angry.

'I was putting the diamonds in here for safety, but never mind that. You kept this picture, all these years.'

'Did I? I hadn't realised.'

'You couldn't have kept it by accident, or brought it all these miles *by accident*.'

'There are a lot of papers in that drawer.'

'Luca, please forget what happened a moment ago. We were both angry and saying things we didn't mean—'

'You, maybe. I don't say things I don't mean. I'm not a sentimentalist, any more than you are.'

She looked at the picture. 'So you didn't keep this on purpose?'

'Good lord, no!'

'Fine, then let's dispose of it.' She tore the picture in half, and then again. 'I'll be going now. The diamonds are there. Goodbye.'

Luca didn't move until she'd walked out. But as soon

as the door had closed behind her he snatched up the four pieces of the picture and tried to put them back together with shaking hands.

Nothing was going right. The look she had surprised on his face, before he could conceal it, had been his undoing. Without meaning to she had breached his defences, and he had instinctively slammed them back into place, bristling with knives.

Deny everything, the picture, its significance, the power it had over him! That was the best way. It was done before he could stop himself, and now he would give anything to call the words back.

He'd thought himself prepared in every detail, but the glamorous sophisticate she had become had taken him by surprise the night before, making him flounder. After that he had made one wrong move after another.

But it wasn't his fault, he reasoned. Her stubbornness hadn't been part of the plan.

He wanted to bang his head against the wall and howl.

CHAPTER FIVE

IN THE early hours of the morning Rebecca heard something being pushed under her door.

She looked down at the envelope without touching it. Then she lifted it and stared longer, while thoughts and fears clashed in her mind.

'Destroy it, unread. If you read it you're embarking on uncharted seas. Play safe.'

She opened the letter.

His handwriting hadn't changed. It was big and confident, an assertion in the face of life. But the words held a hint of something else, almost as though he was confused.

You were right about almost everything. But the day your father arrived wasn't our last meeting. If you want to know about the other one, I'll tell you. Otherwise I won't trouble you again.

Luca

He was playing mind games, was her first thought, but she dismissed it, in fairness. Mind games demanded a subtlety that he didn't have.

She decided to go back to bed and think about it.

An hour later she was knocking on his door. He answered at once.

He was in a white shirt, heavily embroidered down the front, as though he'd spent the evening at a smart function. Now he'd returned and tossed aside his black jacket and torn the shirt open at the neck.

'I'm glad you came,' he growled.

'I want to hear what you have to say, Luca, but then I'm leaving at once.'

'My God, you won't give an inch, will you, even now?'

'No, because whatever you tell me can't really make any difference. How could you ever imagine that it would, after what you did?'

'After what I did?' he echoed. 'What did I do?'

'Oh, please, don't pretend you don't know. We talked about it the first evening. You took my father's money.'

'Naturally. I had every right to it.'

'Of course you did,' she said scornfully. 'After all, you'd given me several months of your valuable time, and I didn't even reward you with a living child. There had to be some recompense for that. But what do you think it did to me to hear my father crowing with delight because you'd lived down to his worst expectations?'

'That I...?' He frowned. 'What did he tell you?'

'That you'd taken his money to go away and never see me again. That's another reason I wouldn't touch those diamonds. Did you think I'd want to take anything from you after you sold me back to him? Besides, you overpaid. I know what those diamonds are worth, and it must be twice what he paid for me. *Or is that interest added on?*'

For a thunderous moment Luca was so silent that she had an eerie feeling that he would never speak again. Then he swore violently, turning away and smashing a fist into the other palm while a stream of invective flowed from him.

'And you've believed that, all these years?' he raged when he turned back.

'What else was I to believe? He showed me the cheque when it had been cashed and returned to him. It was your bank account. Don't pretend it wasn't.'

'Oh, yes, it was mine. He paid me that money, I don't deny it.'

'Then what more is there to say?'

'He lied to you about why. I left because, when Frank had finished, I was sure it was all my fault, the state you were in, the baby's death—I felt guilty about the whole thing.

'Then he had you whisked off to England, to a place I didn't know. I couldn't reach you. I went back to the cottage, and found him there, setting fire to it.'

She stared at him, trying not to believe.

'My father burned our home?' she whispered.

Something flickered across his face.

'Our home. Yes, that's what it was. I'm glad you remembered. He burnt it with his own hands. Luckily there were witnesses. On their evidence he was arrested and put into the cells. He could have faced a long stretch in prison if I hadn't told the police that it was a "misunderstanding" and I wouldn't press charges.'

'Why would you do that?'

His grin flashed out again, cynical, jeering.

'Why, for fifty thousand pounds, of course. That was my price for letting him off. I sold him back his freedom. *Nothing else.*'

'I don't believe it,' she whispered, just as she had done long ago.

'He got caught in the fire himself and burned his arm. Did you never notice that?'

And it came back to her, the memory of Frank arriving one day with his arm in a sling. He said he'd broken it, but months later she'd seen the ugly mark and thought it looked like a burn. When she'd asked him about it, he'd become angry and evasive.

'All these years,' she murmured, 'he told me that you—'

'You heard him offer me money once before,' he reminded her, 'and you heard my reaction.'

'Yes, I remember. He said you'd turned against me when I lost the baby and lost my looks.'

'You never lost them,' he said simply. 'Never. And did you really believe that of me?'

She nodded dumbly.

'You should have had more faith in me, Becky.'

His voice was sad, but not reproachful. He had never blamed her for anything.

'Oh, God,' she whispered. 'All these years, I thought that you—oh, God, oh, God!'

She had thought she'd touched bottom long ago, but now she knew that this was far worse. She went to the window and looked out into the darkness, too confused to think.

'I should have known,' she said at last, 'but I wasn't myself.'

'No, you were never yourself after the day your father came,' he said. 'I saw you once after that. Do you really not remember when I came to the hospital?'

Distressed, she shook her head. 'I always wondered why you never came near me again.'

'Do you think he would let me? He was your father, your next of kin, and I was nothing. If he'd arrived a day later we would have been married, but we weren't, and I had no rights.'

'Yes,' she said, suddenly struck. 'I remember him saying, "Then I'm in time." He meant in time to stop us marrying. But you were the baby's father.'

'Before he came to our door your father had approached the police chief, and got him in his pocket. I was arrested and held in the cells for a week.'

'Dear God! On what charge?'

He shrugged. 'Anything they could think of. It didn't matter, because they never meant to keep me inside for long, just long enough to suit Frank Solway's purpose.

'I thought you were dying. I begged to be allowed to see you, but nobody would listen. And then, at last, your father came to me and told me that the "little bastard" as he called our child, was dead.

'He said it was all my fault, that I'd caused you to lose the child by my "rough behaviour"—'

'But that's not true,' she burst out. 'He was the one who was rough. You didn't fight him back, you just stood there like a rock. I do remember that.'

'Of course I did, because I was afraid to harm you.'

'Then how could you have felt guilty when you knew it wasn't your fault?'

He tore his hair. 'Why does an innocent man ever confess to a crime he hasn't committed? Because they torture his mind until he thinks lies are truth and truth is a lie. I was in such torment, with our child dying, longing for you, not able to get near you, it wasn't hard for him to make me feel that I was entirely to blame.'

She looked at him, torn with pity.

'And then he took me to see you. I thought my chance

had come, that I could take you in my arms and tell you that I loved you. But you weren't in your right mind.'

'I had post-natal depression, very badly, and I think they gave me some strong medication.'

'Yes, I understand that now, but at the time I just walked in and saw you staring into space. I didn't know what had happened. You didn't seem to hear or see me.'

'I didn't,' she breathed. 'I had no idea you'd even been there.'

'I wasn't able to be alone with you. There was your father, and a nurse, in case I ''became violent''. I begged you to hear me. I told you over and over how sorry I was. You just stared at me. *Don't you remember?*'

Dumbly she shook her head. 'I never knew,' she said. 'I must have been completely out of it.'

'And your father knew the state you'd be in while I was there. I wonder what he persuaded the doctor to give you beforehand, to make sure.'

She nodded. She could believe anything of Frank now. 'And he never told me that you came.'

'Of course not. It suited him to have you think I'd callously abandoned you. I went away half-crazy with guilt at the harm I thought I'd done you.'

'It wasn't you, Luca, it wasn't you.'

He regarded her sadly.

'You can tell me that now, but how can you tell the boy I was then? His agony is beyond comfort. Do you remember how it was between us at the very start, how I tried to resist you, for your sake?'

She nodded. 'And I wouldn't let you.'

'My conscience had always troubled me about taking you away from the life you were used to, making you live in poverty.'

'You didn't make me. I chose it when I chose you. And I never felt poor. I felt rich because we loved each other.'

'But I knew I ought to have been stronger. And in the end your father convinced me that the best thing I could do for you was to free you. He said that if I kept trying to ''force myself on you'', you might never recover.'

'He was a bad man,' she said. 'I never fully understood that before.'

Luca nodded.

'I took his money to make myself rich and powerful enough to revenge myself on him. I promised myself we would meet again, but we never did. My business flourished, so I made it my life. Now it's all I know. Becky—'

'I'm Rebecca now,' she said quickly. 'Nobody calls me Becky any more.'

'I'm glad. I want it to be just my name for you. It was special, that time.'

'Yes,' she agreed. 'It was special. But it was another life.'

'But I don't like my life now. Do you?'

'Don't,' she begged, 'don't ask me that kind of question.'

'Why not? If you're happy, you have only to say so. Danvers Jordan is the man of your dreams, right?'

She almost laughed at that. 'Oh, please! Poor Danvers. He's not the man of anyone's dreams.'

'No, he's a dead fish.'

This time she did laugh. 'Your English is still shaky. You mean a cold fish.'

'Whatever. I prefer my version. So life with him isn't blissful. Are you going to marry him?'

'If I decide to, yes! Leave it, Luca. I'm glad to have found out the truth. I've misjudged you, and perhaps we can be friends now. But it doesn't give you the right to question me about my life.'

'Friends? You think we can be friends?'

'It's the best there is.'

He sighed and she thought his shoulders sagged.

'Then let us celebrate our friendship with a drink,' he said.

'All right.' She followed him to the drinks cabinet. 'What do you drink now?' she asked. 'Surely not—?' She named a Tuscan wine, valued for its rough edge.

'No, these days I don't move among people who could appreciate it. You have to be Tuscan.'

'True,' she said. 'Dry sherry, please.'

She watched him pour, watched the deft movements of the big hands that were so powerful, and so tender. They were a rich man's hands now, but no amount of manicuring could hide their suggestion of force. When she looked up she found him looking at her with a soft-ened look on his face.

'Am I very changed?' she asked quietly.

'Your hair's different. It used to be light brown, not as fair as it is now.'

'That isn't what I meant.'

He nodded. 'I know what you meant.'

He stepped closer so that he could look directly into her eyes, not moving for a long moment. Rebecca tried to turn away, but his gaze held her with its fierce inten-sity, and its sadness. She hadn't expected his sadness, and she couldn't cope with it.

'No,' he said at last. 'You haven't changed.'

She gave him a melancholy smile. 'That's not true.'

'I say it is. No, don't move.'

He had laid a hand on her shoulder to keep her there. She stopped and raised her head again, unwilling to meet his eyes but unable to do anything else. At last she could see the connection that spanned the years. The old force and power streamed from him, the confident authority that had been there even when he was penniless. This was Luca as he had been, and as she recognised him now.

Slowly he moved his hand upward so that it brushed against her neck, then her cheek. He seemed almost in a trance, held there by something stronger than himself. She saw his face soften, his expression become almost bewildered, as though something had taken him by surprise.

'Becky,' he murmured, raising his other hand and letting the fingers drift down her face.

The effect was devastating. His touch was so light that she barely felt it, yet it sent through her sensations that she had not known for years. They threatened her, filled her with alarm, yet she could not move.

'Do you remember?' he whispered.

'Yes,' she said sadly. 'I remember.'

If only he would let her go. If only he would never let her go. The feather-light movement of his fingers against her cheek was filling her with a bitter-sweet turmoil, too intense to bear.

As if in a dream she found herself putting up a hand to touch his face. Then she took a sharp breath as she realised how close to danger she had allowed herself to drift.

'Goodbye, Luca,' she said.

His face became set. 'You can't say goodbye to me now.'

'I must. There can't be anything else. It's too late.'

She tried to draw back her hand from his face, but he seized it and turned his head so that his lips lay against the palm.

'Don't,' she whispered. 'It's too late—too late—'

He didn't answer in words, only in the soft scorching of his breath against her palm. She braced herself against it, refusing to yield. He thought he could overcome her, and she would not allow it.

But it was harder than she thought because his touch affected her on two levels. She could cope with the physical excitement that scurried along her nerves, but not the memories of that other, sweeter life.

She was assailed by sensations, not only of pleasure but also of sunshine and happiness. She had forgotten about happiness, what it felt like, even what it was. But now it was there again in visions of a love that had been too intense to last.

The gentle caressing movements of his lips brought back unbearable joy, the nights when she had lain in his arms, revelling in the passion and tenderness of his love.

It had been almost frightening to feel such bliss, but his presence in the bed beside her had been reassuring, and she had fallen asleep against his shoulder, knowing that the next day would bring the same.

Now he was recalling the echoes of that time, and she wanted to avoid them and stay in the safe, chilly cocoon she had built for herself. It was painful to risk leaving that safety, but he was demanding it more insistently with every moment.

'Do you remember?' he murmured. 'Do you remember—?'

'No,' she said urgently. 'I don't want to remember.'

'Don't shut me out, Becky.'

'I must.'

He didn't fight her. He simply withdrew his lips and laid her palm against his cheek again, looking so sad and despairing that she couldn't bear it.

'My darling—' she used the words without knowing '—my darling, please—try to understand—'

'I do,' he said heavily. 'It was a stupid idea, wasn't it?'

'No, it was a beautiful idea, but I guess I have no courage any more.'

'My Becky had courage enough for anything.'

'Long, long ago.'

He looked down, and suddenly she couldn't bear for him to look at her face with the glow of youth gone from it. She pulled his head down to her, so that his lips covered hers.

She knew at once that her body had slept all this time. It wasn't sleeping any more, because he was summoning it to vibrant new life, urgent in its need, carrying her with it despite her sensible self.

His mouth had the same power to coax and demand, but now there was an extra excitement. The boy had gone. The man had a hard edge that coloured all his actions, making her crave to know more of him. She found herself doing what she had sworn not to do, kissing him in a way that urged him on.

He needed no more encouragement to make him extend the kiss into an exploration of her jaw-line, down the length of her neck to the soft place at the base of her throat. Her heart was beating wildly with anticipation, excitement scurrying down from her throat, between her breasts—

'Luca,' she whispered, 'Luca—don't...'

Something in her voice pierced the cloud of desire that pervaded him, and he looked at her intently. There were tears in her eyes.

'Don't cry,' he begged.

'I'm not really. I'm glad it happened. I'll never, never be sorry we met again, and put things right. But I can't go on.'

'Don't give up so soon,' he urged. 'I'm here. You can hold on to me. Becky, take what we have. I don't believe in "too late".'

'I wish I didn't. Let me go, let me go.'

He didn't try to restrain her as she slipped out of his arms, but he watched her all the way to the door.

'You'll come back to me, Becky.'

'No,' she said. 'No, please believe me.'

She slipped out before he could speak again, and she knew that she was fleeing danger. She called herself a coward, but she couldn't help it.

She reached her apartment like a refuge and secured the door behind her, leaning against it, as though fearing an invasion.

She tried to pull herself together. A heavy day faced her, and now she should be sensible and go to bed. But her body was too full of tension and excitement to relax.

She closed her eyes, trying to banish the feel of being held against his hard body, but the more she fought it the more she became aware of it. She'd started something that she had to finish.

All she had to do was go to him now. He might be

asleep, but she knew he wasn't. Her heart told her that he was waiting, listening for the ring of the telephone or the knock on the door. Because he knew, just as she did, that they had not reached the end.

She seized the phone and dialled the penthouse suite. He answered at once, just the one word. 'Yes?' spoken in a voice that was tense and urgent. He knew who it was.

She hung up. She was trembling.

Half an hour passed. He did not ring back.

She slipped quietly out of her apartment, and to the elevator, which drifted up almost soundlessly through the darkened building. At his door she paused only briefly before knocking, and it was opened immediately. He had been waiting for her.

He looked at her for a moment before pulling her fiercely inside and clasping her in his arms so that she was lifted clear off her feet. She could feel the relief that shook him as she put her own arms about him and laid her lips on his.

This was her kiss, with nothing held back. She was too honest to play coy. This had been inevitable from the moment she touched him, because after that she had to touch him again and again. She had to find out if his body was as strong and thrilling as she remembered.

'What do you want?' he whispered.

'I want you,' she murmured back against his mouth. Her hands were at work, pulling open the rest of his buttons, feeling the light sprinkling of hair beneath.

He took over, ripping off the rest of his clothes before ripping off hers. They fell on the bed together, both equally lost in a delirious need to be satiated with each other's bodies.

Rebecca was awake now, every inch of her, vibrant, passionate and hungry, giving him everything she had or was, making feverish demands from the one man who had it in his power to fulfil her.

Luca had always had vigour, but time and experience had added subtlety. He explored her with hands and lips, using both with consummate skill to inflame her senses until she was drawing long, heated, half-moaning breaths.

How could so many years vanish without a trace? How could they still know each other so intimately? She was ready for every move he made, answering with caresses that were skilled in the ways he had always loved, caresses she had offered to no other man, because in her heart she had known they belonged only to him.

As he moved over her she had one last wild moment of doubt. This man was essentially a stranger. But it was no stranger who entered her with the slow, relentless power that had once thrilled her and now thrilled her a thousandfold. Her flesh had slept too long. The awakening was fierce, devastating and total.

She was in his rhythm at once, claiming and releasing him, demanding while she gave, until the mounting pleasure seemed to explode deep within her. Now there was light everywhere, blinding, dazzling, breathtaking. It filled the world, the universe, and it was what she'd been waiting for during all the dead, meaningless years.

CHAPTER SIX

SHE came down from the heights to find herself held tightly in Luca's arms. Perhaps a little too tightly, but she missed the threat of possessiveness because the shattering feeling of sexual release was so powerful, so welcome.

She knew now what she had always suspected, that the reason she was so unresponsive to any other man was that there had always been one man for her. And this was the man.

Luca, blunt, harsh, vengeful, unforgiving: everything she found hard to like. Yet he was the one, because he always had been, and part of her had never changed.

Then he said the wrong thing.

'That was good.'

The hint of calculation chilled her.

'Wasn't it?' he demanded.

Inwardly she withdrew a little, feeling bullied.

'Yes,' she said politely.

'What's the matter?' he asked, just clever enough to know that he'd lost ground, not subtle enough to know why.

'Nothing. I'd like to get up, please.'

'Tell me, first.'

'I want to get up.'

'Tell me!'

'Luca, if you don't release me right now you'll never see me again.'

He released her at once. She was surprised. She hadn't expected the threat to work on this hard man, let alone instantly.

'What is it?' he demanded as she rose and quickly covered her nakedness with a robe. 'What changed?'

'I guess we shouldn't expect too much all at once. Let it go for now.'

Her tone contained a warning and, again to her surprise, he heeded it. After a few moments the silence made her look at him and what she saw melted her heart.

His face showed confusion, and the hurt bewilderment of a child who didn't know what he'd done wrong. It sent her back into his arms.

'Yes, it was good,' she reassured him.

'I still know how to please you?'

'Yes, like nobody else.'

It was the wrong thing to say. His face darkened.

'I don't want to hear about other men.'

'And I'm not going to tell you, but my husband existed. I haven't lived on the shelf all these years, any more than you have. I've been married, so have you.'

'That's enough!' he shouted. 'I don't want to hear it.'

'Fine, you don't have to. You don't have to hear anything you don't want to.' She pulled away from him, looking around for her clothes. Instantly he was beside her.

'Don't go, Becky. I don't want you to go.'

'I think I should,' she said, starting to pull on garments.

'No, you mustn't.' He put his hands out to restrain her, then snatched them back again.

'Don't tell me what I must and mustn't do,' she told him.

'No, I didn't mean that,' he said hurriedly. 'Look, I'm not touching you, but please don't go. Please, Becky. I'll make it right, just tell me what to do, but stay, I beg you.'

His words softened her again. Suddenly they were back in the old days, when this fierce man was putty in her hands, but only hers.

She stopped what she was doing, went over and put her arms around him in consolation. He hugged her back, but gingerly, as though afraid of offending again.

'If you go away, I'm afraid you won't come back,' he said gruffly.

'I will come back. I want to see you again. But take it slowly.'

'I can't,' he admitted. 'I want all of you at once. Stay with me. Come back to bed.'

'No, the hotel will be getting up soon and I don't want to risk being seen.'

'Spend today with me.'

She mentally reviewed the day she'd planned. There were important appointments that she simply couldn't cancel.

'All right,' she said. 'I'll have to make a few calls but—I can do it.'

'We'll go somewhere that we won't be seen by anyone who knows either of us. But you'll have to say where that is. I don't know London.'

'Have you never been here before?' she asked.

'Oh, yes, brief visits, business deals, hotel rooms, travelling in the back of a car to conferences, never seeing anything through the car windows because I was always on the phone. I couldn't tell you how London is different from New York or Milan. If it *is* different.'

'That sounds really dreadful.'

'It's your world too, Becky.'

'Yes, but I get away sometimes.'

'On long country weekends with Jordan?'

'Jordan's a forbidden subject.'

'Suppose I say he isn't?'

'Only a minute ago you told me you didn't want to hear about anyone else.'

'I'll make an exception for Danvers Jordan.'

'But I won't,' she said quietly.

His lips tightened with anger. 'So it has to be on your terms, does it?'

'You said we weren't to talk about the past. They were your terms. I agreed to them. Do you think you can just change them when it suits you? Think again. I'm not dancing on the end of your string.'

'All right, all right,' he said quickly. 'I give in. Your terms.'

She touched his cheek, smiling with rueful tenderness. 'You don't have to give in. That's not what it's all about. But let's not spoil it.'

He took her hand and kissed the palm. 'Anything you say.'

It was like driving at speed around a sharp corner, and only just avoiding the wall. You were left with a desperate sense of relief and a need to rediscover the road you were supposed to be taking.

'So,' she said, determinedly bright, 'you were saying about cities looking the same. Didn't you ever long for the hills of Tuscany?'

He nodded. 'Or any greenery at all. In New York I always tell myself I'll go to Central Park, but I've never been yet. Once I saw some trees as I was driving through

London, and told the driver to stop the car. But then the phone rang. I was late for a meeting, so I told him to start it again.'

'Where were you when this happened?'

He thought for a moment. 'We'd just passed a huge round red building. I think the driver said they gave concerts there.'

'The Albert Hall. The trees you saw were in Hyde Park. Let's go there, then.'

'Fine.' He reached for the telephone.

'What are you doing?'

'Calling my driver.'

She placed her hand firmly over his. 'We're not calling your driver, or mine.'

'Aren't we?'

'Nope. We're going to go out and hunt for a taxi, and then nobody will know where we've gone.'

That turned it into a conspiracy, and suddenly everything was fun. They took the elevator down almost all the way, and Luca got out one floor from the last. Anyone who happened to be in the lobby saw him walk out of the hotel alone. None of them saw him turn the corner and meet up with Rebecca, who'd gone down the back stairs, left by the kitchen entrance, and was already hailing a taxi.

It was little more than a mile to Hyde Park, but the congestion had already started, and it was three-quarters of an hour before they arrived.

'Green,' Luca said, looking around him with joy. 'Grass. Trees.'

He took her hand and began to walk, across the grass, and she hurried with him. It touched her that Luca, reared amidst savagely beautiful scenery, could still find pleasure in this place with its manicured lawns. It told a whole story about how cut off he'd become from his roots.

'What's that?' He had stopped abruptly at the sight of a large stretch of water, snaking out of sight in both directions. 'A river?'

'No, it's a long, thin lake,' she laughed. 'It's called the Serpentine.'

'And we can take a boat. I see them over there.'

'Come on, then. I haven't been on a boat on the Serpentine for years.'

They hired a rowing boat, big enough for her to sit facing him in a cushioned seat. Luca took the oars and began to pull on them strongly, while Rebecca leaned back, enjoying the chance to relax and simply watch him. After the turmoil of the last few days it was good to think of nothing but the beautiful day, and the pleasure of being on the water. She fixed her eyes on him and let her thoughts drift.

But this was a mistake because in a haze of drowsy contentment she found herself looking at his hands, remembering last night. He had touched her in so many ways, sometimes gently, intimately, sometimes fiercely, and she had responded ecstatically to all of them.

And the way she'd touched him back—she found it hard to recall details now. She had explored and celebrated him with reckless joy, revelling in his instant response, demanding more. She had not known herself capable of such vigorous possessiveness.

Her mind drifted back to her ex-husband, the man she thought of as 'poor Saul'. He'd been entitled to pity because she'd had less than half a heart to give him, and almost no passion. He'd been infatuated and she'd yielded to his eagerness from hope of finding a purpose in her life.

But she had disappointed him, and in his bitterness he'd called her 'the iceberg'. The kindest thing she had ever done for him was to leave him.

She returned from her reverie to find that Luca's eyes were on her, and he was smiling faintly.

'What is it?' she asked. 'Why are you looking at me like that?'

'I'm trying to behave like a gentleman, and not succeeding. The truth is that all I can think of is how badly I want to make love to you.'

The words 'make love' were like a signal, starting a slow-burning fuse inside her. It was only a few hours since she'd risen, satiated, from his bed, yet with just two words she'd become ready for him again. It was shameless, and slightly shocking. It was also thrilling, and deeply, searingly enjoyable.

'You'd better start rowing back, then,' she said. 'Careful! Don't upset the boat.'

They rocked violently all the way back to the shore and climbed out with such urgency that they nearly ended up in the water.

'Where's the nearest exit?' he demanded.

'Over there.'

They made it in double-quick time, but when they reached the street an obstacle met them.

'Oh, no!' Rebecca groaned. 'Isn't the morning rush over yet?'

'Your traffic jams are as bad as Rome,' Luca complained. 'Nothing's moving.'

'It'll take hours to get back to the Allingham,' Rebecca said.

He gripped her hand tighter. 'We don't have hours,' he said firmly. 'Where is the nearest hotel?'

She began to laugh. 'Luca, we can't—'

'Becky, I swear to you that if you don't direct me to an hotel I shall make love to you here and now, on the grass.'

There was a note in his voice that told her he might actually mean it. There was simply no knowing what this determined man might do. It made him thrilling.

'I'm warning you,' he said, slipping his arms around her.

'Stop it! Behave!'

'Find us a hotel, then, quickly.'

'If we cross the road and take that turning there are quite a few in that street up there.'

Crossing the road was easy, since none of the traffic was moving. They found themselves in a street of small private hotels, some of which had notices bearing the word 'Vacancies' in the window. Luca dashed into the first one they came to.

This was a different world from the whispering luxury of the Allingham. There was a small hall, with a cubby-hole for the receptionist, who was absent. Luca had to ring the bell twice, and the second time he did so with such force that a harassed-looking woman emerged from the rear, looking indignant.

'I'd like a room, please,' Luca said. 'Immediately.'

'It isn't noon,' the woman said, with a glance at the clock on the wall that showed half-past eleven.

'Is that important?'

'If you take possession before twelve I'm afraid I have to charge you for two days.'

'How much is the room per night?' Luca asked, breathing hard.

'Seventy pounds, per person, per night. You would be requiring a double room, I take it?'

'Yes,' said Luca, almost beside himself. 'We would like a double room.'

'Then that would be a hundred and forty pounds for one night, so perhaps you would care to wait half an hour, and only pay for one night, which will be cheaper.'

'That's not a good idea,' Rebecca said hastily. 'We'll take it now, thank you.'

'Very well. Name?'

'Mr and Mrs Smith,' Rebecca said promptly.

The receptionist showed, by raised eyebrows, exactly what she thought of that.

'I see. Well, we operate a liberal regime here, although it did seem to me that this was a foreign gentleman—'

'He's a foreign gentleman called Smith,' said Rebecca, poker-faced.

'Well, if one of you would sign here...'

Rebecca hastily seized the pen. Luca was in no mood to remember what name he was supposed to be signing.

The room, when they finally took possession of it, was basic but adequate. Luca shut the door firmly, locked it and turned to her swiftly.

But she was ahead of him, tossing her clothes aside, her eyes gleaming with anticipation.

'Come on,' she said. 'Slow coach.'

He needed no further encouragement, matching her for speed, until they were both ready to fall onto the bed and claim each other with feverish intensity. No subtlety.

No pretence that this was anything but frantic, exuberant lust, relished for its own sake, with no holds barred.

She wanted him inside her. She'd wanted that since he'd left her only a few hours ago, and when she had what she wanted she kept tight hold of him, arching against him insistently and looking up into his face with a smile that made him smile back.

It was she who decided that the moment had come, moving faster, and then faster.

'Wait,' he told her.

'No,' she said simply.

He tried to hold her back but his own desire was uncontrollable, and they finished triumphantly together, laughing and crowing with triumph.

When he had the strength to move, Luca sat up, and blew out his cheeks. 'I've been thinking of this ever since—since I got up this morning.'

'So have I,' she said, relieved at being able to admit it. 'Luca, I don't know who I am any more. I have never been like this in all my life.'

He raised himself from his back, rolled over and looked down at her nakedness with appreciative eyes.

'Shall I tell you who you are?' he asked, sliding his hand over her breasts again.

She chuckled. 'Does it involve vigorous exercise?'

'It might. Unless you're tired.'

'Who's tired? It's early yet.' She reached for him, letting him know with gestures what she wanted of him, and the pleasure was all given back to her, again and again.

As they lay together afterwards she said dreamily, 'I'll bet it's past noon by now.'

'It's three in the afternoon,' he said.

'Ah, well, it can't be helped,' she said drowsily, not knowing what she meant by this.

'Why did you tell them that we were Mr and Mrs Smith?'

'I had to tell them something.'

'But what did she mean about a liberal regime?'

'In the old days, when people weren't as free as they are now, people who wanted to be together used to book into a hotel under the name of Mr and Mrs Smith. So whenever you told a hotel that your name was Smith— well—'

'They knew you were unmarried lovers,' he finished.

'Something like that.'

'And that's why she gave us such a funny look?'

'Yes. She knew exactly why we couldn't wait until noon.'

Luca began to laugh, burying his face against her neck and shaking. And she too laughed, because it was really incredibly funny. For years there had been no laughter in the world. Now there was nothing else but laughter and joy, pleasure and fulfilment, the one leading to the other, then back again, and round in an endless circle of delight.

All strain and tension seemed to fall away, leaving her relaxed and gloriously content. When Luca raised his head she saw that it was the same with him.

'I could go to sleep now,' he said, laying his head back on her shoulder.

'Mmm, lovely.'

But the shrill of his cellphone brought them back to reality. With a grimace he swung himself off the bed.

'I should have switched it off,' he said. 'Hello,

Sonia—no, I'm not at the hotel for the moment—nothing wrong, just a change of plan. Anything urgent?'

He yawned as he listened. Rebecca too yawned. It felt pleasant to lie here, drifting into a light doze. Luca's voice reached her faintly.

'All right, there's no problem, but he's got to come down on the price, or no deal. Sure, I know what he was hoping for, but he's not going to get it. I can go else-where, but he can't.'

For half an hour she floated happily in and out of consciousness.

'There's no point in talking any more, Sonia. He and I have done business before. He knows I mean what I say. Now, about the future—I won't be at the Allingham for a few days. You can reach me on this phone, but not too often, OK?'

He hung up. Rebecca slowly sat up in the bed.

'Where are you planning to be for the next few days, Luca?'

'Here. With you.'

'And what about my appointments? My job?'

'Becky, I can imagine how your appointments read. Lunch with this one, drinks with that one, supervising some hotel function, attending a conference. How am I doing?'

'Pretty good.'

'And how vital is any of it? Nobody needs that lunch, that social occasion. Conferences are hot air. The deals depend on cold cash, nothing else, and they're all sewn up before anyone arrives.'

'You're saying that I'm just playing at doing a job,' she said indignantly.

'No, I'm not. My own job is just as full of froth. It's

the way of the world these days. I escape it whenever I
can, and the skies don't fall. Will they fall if *you* take a
few days off?'

She was about to say that it was impossible when she
realised that he was only voicing her own recent
thoughts. Golden, glittering and hollow; that was how
she'd seen her life as she arrived at Philip Steyne's house
that fateful night.

'I could have a word with my assistant,' she said.
'She's very good.'

She didn't mention that she would have to break a
date with Danvers, but that would have happened anyway. After what had occurred between her and Luca
there was no way she could maintain the pretence that
she and Danvers were an item.

All the way back to the hotel she thought about what
she would say to him. Entering the Allingham alone, she
went to her office and made the necessary arrangements
with her assistant, an efficient young woman who could
hardly contain her delight at being left in charge.

'By the way, there's a message from Mr Jordan,' she
said. 'He has to be away for a few days, maybe a week,
he wasn't sure. He says he'll call you when he gets
back.'

'Fine,' Rebecca said, torn between relief that she
could defer the problem, and dismay that it was going
to drag on.

But perhaps this was best, she thought as she slipped
out into the street with a suitcase. Now she could forget
everything but enjoying a holiday.

The next few days felt like the first true holiday of
her life. Hidden away with Luca in the shabby little hotel, she felt as though she were living in the sun.

He was a tireless lover, who could bring her to the heights again and again, and still want her. And she, who had long ago decided that the traumas of her youth had left her cold and unresponsive, could be ready for him at any moment of the night or day, except that night and day were indistinguishable.

The hotel had no Room Service so they ate burgers at a café around the corner, always hurrying back to fall into bed. For four days they loved and slept, slept and loved. In fact, they did everything except talk. But at the time that didn't seem very important.

One morning Rebecca came out of the shower to find Luca just hanging up the phone, looking exasperated.

'I've got to go back to Rome,' he said. 'One of my deals is unravelling, and I need to be there.'

She tried to smile, but the turmoil inside her was alarming. He was going away, and she couldn't stand it.

'Oh, well,' she said lightly. 'It's been great, but we knew it couldn't last forever.'

'We have to give up this room,' he agreed, 'but I'll be back in a few days.'

She'd got her second wind now and could smile.

'Hey, I won't count on it. You may need to stay.'

He was still sitting on the bed, and as she passed him he caught both her hands in his, looking up into her face.

'I'll be back in a few days,' he said. 'I don't think I could stand it for longer.'

'I suppose I should be glad you're going,' she said with a faint smile. 'It'll give me a chance to catch up with real life.'

'Real?' He regarded her with raised eyebrows. 'This hasn't been real?'

She caressed his hair. 'You know what I mean.'

He grinned. Laughing, she leaned down and kissed him.

'I must try to get my mind back on my job,' she said a few moments later. 'And I suppose I ought to speak to Danvers, just to tell him that what little there was between us is all over. Don't worry about him.'

'I won't,' he said simply. Then he gave a broad grin. 'Danvers Jordan doesn't worry me at all.'

She thought he meant that after the last few days he was riding high on pride and sexual confidence.

Afterwards she was to wonder how she could have been so stupid.

CHAPTER SEVEN

LUCA was away nearly a week, during which he called
her ten times. She lived for those calls. It grew harder
to pretend that she didn't, and after a while she wasn't
pretending at all.

She didn't know what to call this feeling. Somehow
love did not seem the right word. The bond between
them had mysteriously survived years and distance. Now
she could think of nothing else but him. Her whole life
seemed concentrated around the thought of him, his next
call, the likely date of his return.

And yet, for reasons she did not understand, she re-
sisted calling it love.

Two days before he was due home she was on duty
at a hotel reception. It lasted only two hours, yet the
time seemed interminable, because these days she could
no longer take such occasions seriously. She wondered
if she would ever do so again.

Smiling mechanically at someone who had claimed
her attention and seemed determined to keep her forever,
she managed to look around the room and, to her surprise, noticed Danvers on the far side. She hadn't known
that he was back, and that was strange because he was
normally so punctilious.

The sight of him made her realise how little she'd
thought of him while he was away, so absorbed had she
been in Luca. If Danvers had not contacted her, neither
had she contacted him. Soon she must see him and ex-

plain why their relationship, such as it had ever been, was over.

At last she managed to bring the present conversation to an end and made her way through the crowd, noticing that Danvers was deep in conversation with a young woman. When he became aware of Rebecca a sudden alert look came over his face, and she could almost believe that he met her with reluctance.

'Rebecca,' he said with a forced smile. 'How nice to see you.' As if she were a casual acquaintance.

'Good evening, Danvers.' She smiled at the young woman. A strange feeling was growing in her.

'Ann, this is Mrs Hanley, the Allingham's public-relations officer. Ann is my secretary at the bank.'

The two women greeted each other politely. Danvers looked around in the crowd.

'Is Montese with you?' he asked.

'No. Why should he be?'

'I just wondered. Ann, would you mind...?'

The other woman slipped away, leaving Rebecca looking at Danvers in a puzzled way.

'Did you have a good trip?' she asked.

'Yes, it went very well.'

'Have you been back long?'

'Three days.'

Three days. And he hadn't called her. That was more baffling than painful.

'You normally don't wait that long to call me,' she said, trying to sound light.

'Oh, please, Rebecca, don't pretend. You know perfectly why I haven't been in touch. Don't tell me that you mind.'

She frowned. 'Danvers, I—'

'It would have been quite enough for you to tell me yourself, you know. You didn't have to send in the heavy squad.'

'I don't know what you mean.'

'I mean Luca Montese claiming ownership like some tribal warlord.'

'Ownership of what?'

'You, of course. What else? He left me in no doubt that unpleasant things would happen if I didn't back off.'

'What? Danvers, I don't believe that. It can't be true. You must have misunderstood.'

'Believe me, when Montese sets out to make his point there is no misunderstanding. You belong to him. Keep off. That was the message.'

'I most certainly do not belong to him.'

'Tell him. He thinks you do.'

'Danvers, are you saying he actually threatened you with physical violence?'

'Nothing so obvious. He didn't need to. He's a man who knows everything.'

'About what?'

'About everything and everyone. He knew all about me, things I thought dead and buried.'

'Things the bank wouldn't like?' Rebecca asked. It was a shot in the dark but she knew it had gone home when she saw his face tighten.

'It was just a piece of foolishness and it was long ago. There was no harm done. Nobody lost out. The rules were laxer in those days anyway. But if it came to light now—well, anyway, I'm not taking chances.'

She regarded him curiously. 'I suppose it didn't occur to you to defend your right to me?'

'Get real, darling. I've got a career to make. He'd

never take his claws out of me. He had a complete dossier. Probably got one on you as well.'

'Don't talk nonsense,' she said, but her voice was uncertain.

'Rebecca, don't be naïve. You don't have the first idea what this man is really like. He's hard, dangerous, ruthless. And whatever there is between you, he'll be as ruthless to you as anyone else. Ann, darling! Over here.'

'Yes, you've talked to me longer than is safe, haven't you?' Rebecca said with a touch of contempt, and walked away without a backward glance.

She had to wait two days for Luca to return, and they were the longest two days of her life. Sometimes she told herself that what she was thinking could not possibly be true.

Her recent time with him had been glorious, a brilliant light in the grey that was her normal life. But she knew that the bliss was due entirely to their blazing sexual compatibility.

There was always one more loving to come, one more fierce, shattering pleasure to fill her world and drive out thoughts she didn't want to think.

Lost in a haze of physical delight, she'd had little time to consider the personality of the man. Or perhaps she had chosen to look away, secretly aware that she would find too many things that she would not like.

She had heard him on the phone, giving Sonia his instructions, talking of his associates or his rivals with a blunt disregard of anything except coming out on top. She had brushed the knowledge aside, telling herself that he swam in shark-infested waters, and must survive by using tough weapons.

She had refused to see what kind of man Luca had

turned into, but the knowledge had always been there like an echo at the back of her mind.

Now, she knew instinctively that what Danvers had said was true. She waited only to hear it from Luca's own lips.

She arranged with the desk to inform her as soon as he returned to the hotel, and the call came late in the evening. Two minutes later she was knocking at the door of his suite.

His face broke into a smile at the sight of her.

'I was just calling you,' he said. 'This is wonderful.'

He drew her into the room, shutting the door behind her and taking her into his arms.

As always, the sheer physical explosiveness of his kiss changed the world, driving out everything that was not him. With his lips caressing hers purposefully it was hard to believe that anything else mattered. Why stir up trouble? Why not just give in to her body's need?

She tried not to yield to such thoughts.

'Luca...'

But he was already removing her clothes and she lacked the will to stop him. He could ignite her excitement with a gesture, a kiss, a touch of his finger on her face. After that it was like a chain reaction, flowing like liquid fire, unstoppable until it had reached the inevitable end.

When she was naked she saw a look in his eyes that melted her, as though he was seeing her nakedness for the first time, and was astounded by it. That was one thing about Luca, she realised hazily. He was never blasé. His delight in her now was the same as long ago. After nearly a week his urgency was almost uncontainable, and so was her own, she discovered, secretly shocked.

What she knew of him made no difference to her desire to have him, and that was the scariest thing of all. She gave him back pleasure for pleasure, delight for delight, knowing that her body was responding without her mind's consent. It was like losing herself and being unable to prevent it. Then the thought was lost in the sexual release he could give her.

Luca, holding on to her quivering body, sensed something different about her. It confused him even while it obscurely pleased him. He had done the right thing in seeking her out, for she was like no other woman. What a life they would have!

When it was over he propped himself up on one elbow and looked down at her with frank pleasure. Rebecca had always enjoyed that expression in his eyes, but now the thoughts and fears that she had pushed aside came crowding back to her. And with them came the troubled knowledge that he had overcome her resistance without even trying. He had too much power over her, and if she didn't resist now it would be too late.

'I like you best when you're like this,' he said, smiling and running a hand over her nakedness.

'No.' She seized his hand and held it. 'I want to talk.'

'Can't it wait?'

'It's waited too long. I meant to talk as soon as I arrived but—well—'

'But we want each other too much for talking,' he finished for her. 'Does anything else matter?'

'Yes, I think it does. Something's happened that we have to discuss.'

'All right. Tell me.'

'I was at a hotel reception a couple of days ago, and I saw Danvers. He tried to avoid me.'

Looking into his eyes, she saw a look of wariness, and her heart sank.

'Is it true what he told me? That you warned him off?'

He shrugged. 'OK, OK. Yes, I did.'

With a violent movement she rose from the bed and began dressing quickly. Suddenly it seemed indecent for him to see her naked.

She had expected the answer, but somehow that didn't prepare her for the brutal reality. Now she needed to set a distance between them. He too rose and dressed, glancing at her with a dark expression.

When she was finished she turned on him, her eyes kindling. 'You dared to dictate who I could see or not see?'

'I needed a clear field to get near you, so I drove off the competition. Don't be so tragic about it. Men do it every day.'

'But how many men are like you, Luca? Danvers said you threatened him with something in his past. You'd compiled a dossier. That must have taken some time. You knew about him before you ever came here, didn't you? And not just him.'

He was watching her carefully, like a man trying to guess which way a cat would spring. How strange, she thought, that she had blinded herself to that calculating look in his eyes. How often had it been there, and she would not let herself see it?

'The clue was there on the evening we met,' she said quietly, 'but I ignored it.'

'What clue?'

'You immediately called me "*Mrs* Hanley". Of

course, you might have worked out that that was my married name, or someone might have told you, but actually you already knew, didn't you?'

He didn't answer.

'Tell me, Luca, was that meeting really a surprise to you?'

'No,' he admitted.

'You knew who I was. You knew I'd been married, and my married name. You knew everything before I arrived at the house, didn't you?'

'Yes.'

'In other words, you had a dossier on me too.'

He shrugged. 'Does it matter?'

'Does it—? Of course it matters. All this time I thought we just chanced to bump into each other, and you let me think it. But you'd planned everything. Calculated everything. You deceived me.'

'I never deceived you,' he shouted. 'Not you.'

'Just everybody else?'

He shrugged.

'What does anyone else matter? I wanted to find you, and I found you.'

'But how? You had me hunted down like a block of shares, didn't you? Luca Montese, financier and predator, gets the prey in his sights and moves in for the kill.'

'If you want to find someone you put it in the hands of an expert. What's wrong with that?'

'Nothing, if you'd told me. But you let me think it was just life working out naturally.'

'Life never works out. You have to tell it where you want it to go, and then make sure it does. Your father would have said the same.'

'Don't. It makes you sound like him, and I don't want that.'

'Then tell me what you do want,' he said.

'I want to turn back the clock to before this happened,' she said desperately. 'You were never this kind of man before.'

'You're wrong,' he said harshly. 'I was always this kind of man. You just never saw it.'

'Then I'm glad I never saw it,' she cried. 'Because I couldn't have loved you as a bully and a schemer, twisting people, twisting facts, anything as long as you get your own way. That's what my father used to do, and I can't bear it. If you've turned into him, it spoils what we had then and I wanted to keep it.'

'We can't keep it,' he shouted. 'It was destroyed long ago. We've created something else, and that's what we have to hold on to. Don't endanger it by brooding about things that don't matter.'

'Don't matter?' she echoed. 'You don't know what matters and what doesn't. You say we've created something else, but what have we created? What *can* it be when it's based on lies?'

'I had to find you, Becky. I *had* to. I couldn't let anything stand in my way.'

'No, nothing stands in your way, does it, Luca? Not honour or fair dealing or decent behaviour, or other people's feelings. Nothing. I'm seeing a lot of things now.'

'I had to find you,' he repeated stubbornly. 'It was more important than you'll ever know.'

'So why not be honest? All those pretty delusions you fed me, about fate! And it was a lie because you set it all up.'

She looked at him curiously.

'Luca, just how much did you know about me, that night at Philip Steyne's house?'

'A good deal,' he admitted unwillingly.

'Did you know I was going to be there?'

'I was pretty sure. I knew Jordan was going to be there, and you were seeing him, so it figured. I also knew you worked for the Allingham, so I was bound to find you sooner or later.'

'You knew I worked for the Allingham?' she echoed. 'Is that why you bought shares?'

'Yes.'

She gave a wild laugh. 'All that, just to find me again?'

'Does it matter how it happened, as long as we found each other again?'

'But we haven't found each other, can't you see that? No, you can't, can you? And that means we're further apart than we ever were. At one time you would never have deceived me.'

He flinched, and she knew she'd struck home.

'I would have told you the truth eventually,' he growled. 'But this was important. I couldn't take chances. It has to be you, it can't be anyone else.'

'Don't tell me you've been pining with love for me all these years. You married, remember.'

'Yes, and it was no good.'

'It must have been good for part of the time.'

'She had a son by a damned hairdresser,' he snapped.

'So she was unfaithful, but that doesn't mean—'

'Six years and never a hint of a baby. Barren for me, fertile for him. *Dear God!*'

He said the last words violently, his face distorted. Rebecca stared at him, aghast. She had partly known this from Nigel Haleworth, but now a dreadful suspicion had come into her mind. It was impossible. She was imagining crazy things. In a moment he would say something that proved it couldn't be true.

He was still talking, but more to himself than her.

'I had a child once. She died, but she need not have done. She would have been fifteen.'

'I know,' she said, stony-faced.

'Fifteen! Think of it.'

'I think of it all the time,' she cried. 'I think of it every year on what would have been her birthday, and I never stop grieving. But we can't bring her back to life.'

'But we can create new life. You and I. What we've done once we can do again.'

'Luca, what are you saying?'

He turned on her, eyes blazing with intensity.

'I want a child, Becky. Your child.'

'And that was in your mind when you searched for me?' she asked slowly.

'Yes. It's important.'

'I can imagine it would be. And now, of course, I realise why you didn't tell me at once.'

'I could hardly do that,' he said, misled by her reasonable tone.

'Of course not,' she agreed. 'It wouldn't be easy to say, would it? ''Good evening Rebecca, nice to see you after fifteen years, and will you be my brood mare?'''

'It's not like that—'

'It's exactly like that, you cold-blooded, insensitive, calculating machine. Luca, I'll never forgive you for this, and if you can't see why, then you've moved further down the wrong path than any man I've ever known.'

'All right, all right, I haven't handled it well, but—'

'Listen to yourself!' she cried, tormented beyond endurance. 'Handled it! Do you know how often you use that phrase? That's how life is to you, something to be "handled". Do this, and everything will work out according to the Luca Montese book of sharp practice. Do that, and it'll all go wrong, because you weren't ruthless enough. Well, nobody could accuse you of not being ruthless enough, but I promise you it's gone wrong. And it'll never be right again.'

'You're determined to misunderstand everything I say.'

'On the contrary, I've understood only too well. You want a son—'

'I want *your* son. Yours. Nobody else's. No other woman's child would mean the same to me.'

But her face was unforgiving.

'You mean,' she said bitterly, 'that I've already proved myself with you, so I'm a safer bet than a stranger?'

He paled. 'That's a hard way of putting it.'

'Tell me another way that comes anywhere near the truth.'

She turned away and began to stride the room.

'I can't believe myself. To think I actually let you touch me after what I heard from Danvers.'

'But you did,' he said harshly. 'Doesn't that prove how strong the bond between us still is?'

'No, it only proves we're good in bed together. There's no true bond between us now, Luca. Just sex, sex and more sex. And then more sex. You're the most sexually exciting man I've ever known, or ever will know, and it makes quite a bond, I admit. In fact it's such a wonderful bond that I've told myself fairy tales about it ever since we met again. I've tried so hard to believe that it was enough, and I suppose that for your purposes it *is* enough.'

'Becky, don't—'

'Why not? It's the truth. If you want to impregnate a woman so that you can flaunt her fertility to the world, then you don't need love or emotional connection. Cold, heartless lust will do the job just as well, won't it, Luca?'

'Stop it, Becky,' he said savagely.

'Sure, I'll stop it. I've made my point. Sex isn't enough, even when it's as good as ours. But it's all we have. Perhaps it's all we ever had.'

'*No!*' It was a cry of agony. 'No, that isn't true. Never say it, do you hear?'

'Still giving me orders. Still trying to arrange everyone like pawns on your chess board. Don't worry. You'll never have to hear me say anything again.

'Go away, Luca. Leave the Allingham, sell your shares, go back to Italy, and tell yourself that you're well rid of that awkward woman who wouldn't fall into line. Find a woman you can be honest with—if you can take the risk.'

She was gone while he was still too stunned to speak. The slam of the door was a deliberate act of contempt.

The phone rang. It was Sonia, with a mountain of problems that had sprung up the moment he left Italy. He suppressed the impulse to slam down the telephone and pursue Rebecca, and was glad, afterwards. In her present mood it would have been the worst thing he could have done.

Despite her words his mind persisted on the old fixed track. He had handled it badly. The best thing was to give her time to cool down, then they would talk. She would see things his way. It was all a question of how you handled it.

He worked until late in the evening, talking to Sonia, sending emails. By the time he logged off the internet he was about half a million richer than he had been at the start.

He was wondering if enough time had passed for him to call her when he heard a knock on his door. He opened it, only half believing that it could be her. But it was.

She gave him a half-smile, as though considering whether to tell him a secret.

'May I come in?'

'Of course.' He stood back, trying to decipher her mood. 'Does this mean you're going to let me explain?'

'No, let's not bother. We both know the score.' She shrugged and turned to him, laughing. 'We were keeping score in different ways, that's all.'

He grinned. 'We can put that right.'

The phone rang. He muttered something under his breath as he snatched it up. 'Sonia, not now—'

'Finish what you have to do,' Rebecca said lightly. 'There's no hurry.'

But he did hurry, because there was a note in her voice that was unfamiliar to him and he wanted to know more. He had no idea what she was up to, but he was willing to find out.

He disposed of the call fast, and turned to find that Rebecca had closed all the curtains. She was standing there, arms folded across the buttoned jacket of her trouser suit, smiling at him in a way that could have only one meaning.

He took her into his arms, feeling her lean towards him. As her arms went around his neck he began to unbutton her jacket and immediately realised that she wore nothing underneath.

He had never before known her so bold and daring, and accepted the implied invitation with eagerness.

When she was naked she took his hand and led him to bed, falling onto it and opening her arms. As soon as he went into them she closed them around him with a movement that was almost as predatory as his own.

Their times together had given her a new confidence, and now she could guide and even direct him, urging him on to what pleased her. Her own caresses were almost casual in their skill, arrogant in their assumption that power lay with her, and she could please him at will. She succeeded beyond his wildest expectations.

Rebecca had an eerie sensation of being two people. One of them was floating above all this, looking down at the woman who seemed so immersed in making passionate love with this man, and who was actually detached from him, from everything that was happening, and—terrifyingly—from herself.

And she was cold, so cold that it was a wonder that the man didn't turn to ice in her arms.

Luca caught a glimpse of her eyes and thought he detected a look of desperation. Then it was gone and all he knew was that she was surging against him, crying incoherently with pleasure.

His own pleasure was shattering, driven to new heights by her responsiveness, and by the skills that had lain, hitherto unsuspected, in her slim body. He guessed that she was not making love, but making sex, and it left him gasping and close to exhaustion.

The end came when she decided. When she pushed him gently away from her he lay, his head turned on the pillow, unwilling to take his eyes from her.

She drew herself up in bed and sat there like a shameless nymph, letting him appreciate her glorious nakedness. She was laughing.

'That was good,' she said.

Failing to pick up the echo, he said, 'Yes, it was.'

His cellphone rang. He grabbed for it, switched it off and tossed it away onto the floor. That made her laugh even more.

'What is it?' he asked, laughing with her but not knowing why.

'Nothing, just a private joke.'

'So tell me.'

'Leave me my secrets.'

'When will you tell me?'

She put her hands behind her head and lay back on the pillow. 'You'll know in time,' she said. 'Go to sleep.'

He did so, letting himself drift away in a blissful haze, until he fell into the deep sleep of total physical contentment.

Rebecca watched him, the laughter gone from her face. Now the look of desperation he'd briefly glimpsed was back in her eyes, and when her tears began to fall she did not wipe them away.

CHAPTER EIGHT

Luca awoke with only one thought. He had won. Again. As always.

She had tried to leave him and couldn't. She belonged to him again, just as he'd planned, and now there was nothing standing in the way of their future together.

He turned over, reaching for her, wanting to share warmth with her, to see in her eyes his own knowledge that they belonged together.

She wasn't there.

He listened for the sound of the shower, but there was only silence from the bathroom. Her clothes were gone. She was gone.

He dialled her room, but the ringing went unanswered.

No matter. She'd gone out for a walk, to contemplate what had happened between them. She was planning for their future. He told himself this while his mind frantically tried to shut out his fears.

He called her cellphone, but it was switched off. Next he tried Nigel Haleworth, the hotel manager, attempting to make his voice sound casual.

'Nigel, sorry to call so early, but I need to contact Mrs Hanley. She doesn't seem to be in her room. Do you know when she'll be back?'

'Funny you should ask that,' came Nigel's bluff voice. 'I've just had her on the line, saying she won't be back.'

'Of course she will, she...' Luca checked himself on the verge of an indiscretion. Since he couldn't say... 'She

114

just gave me the night of my life', he substituted, 'She has her job here.'

'Not any more, apparently. She's given in her notice and simply walked out, which is a bit inconvenient, actually. She should have let me have some notice, instead of just clearing out her things and going.'

'Where is she now?' His throat was tight. His voice sounded strange to his own ears.

'Didn't say.'

'But suppose mail should come for her?'

'She said she'd be in touch about that. Look, why don't you call Danvers Jordan? They were practically engaged, so he's bound to know. In fact, he's probably the one who wanted her to leave. Young love, eh?'

Luca ground his teeth, but this was no moment to tell the manager that his information was out of date. He tried Rebecca's cellphone again, but it was no real surprise to find it still switched off. He knew now that she meant business.

A knock at his door revealed a hotel messenger with mail that had been delivered for him at Reception. He sorted through the envelopes quickly, automatically setting aside those that looked important, although none of them felt important at this moment.

Then he stopped as he came to one with Rebecca's handwriting. He suddenly seemed paralysed. He did not want to read it, in case it said what he knew it would.

Then he tore it open and read,

Luca, my dear,
Last night was a goodbye. I couldn't bear to leave you finally without one last reminder of the best there was between us. I know now I can't love you again.

*Please don't blame me for that, but treasure the
sweetest memories, as I shall.
Goodbye,*

Becky

His first reaction was denial. It was impossible that he
had found her and lost her, and that she had simply
vanished without giving him the chance to bar her way.

He kept pain at bay by fixing on details. It chilled him
to think of the smirks in Reception as she handed this
in at the desk when she'd left. They would guess.

But then he studied the envelope, and saw that it had
a cancelled stamp and a postmark. It had come in the
mail, which meant it must have been posted yesterday.

Suddenly all the strength seemed to drain out of him
as he realised that she had made love to him last night
in the knowledge of that letter already written, and beyond recall.

With strength gone, he had no defence against pain,
and he found himself caught up in it like a man caught
in heavy waves, being smashed against rocks. There was
no way out, no protection, just suffering to be endured.

At last anger came to his rescue. It was the talisman
by which he silenced all other feeling and he invoked it
now against his enemy.

He was waiting at Danvers Jordan's office before the
working day began.

'Just tell me if you know where she is,' he said dan-
gerously as soon as he'd closed the door.

'I don't know what you're talking about,' Danvers
said coolly.

'I hope, for your sake, that's true. I'll ask you one
more time. Where is Rebecca?'

'Look, if I knew, I'd tell you. She's nothing to me any more. You're welcome to her. But she seems to have finished with the pair of us.'

He barely controlled a sneer as he surveyed Luca.

'I did what you demanded, and left you a clear field. It doesn't seem to have done you much good, but what did you expect? Rebecca is a lady. Of course she didn't hang around once she'd enjoyed her "bit of rough".'

At one time Luca would have knocked him down for that, without a second thought. But now he couldn't move. When he finally managed to get some strength into his limbs it was only enough to walk away.

He didn't look where he was going, for his attention was fixed on the grinning clown in his head. It hooted with derisive laughter, mocking him for his weakness in swallowing an insult, and saying that it was all her fault. The habit of not doing what she wouldn't like had returned at a fatal moment. And he was the clown.

Travelling was the best way to escape, because a woman could convince herself she was headed somewhere, instead of going around in circles.

Just who that woman was Rebecca couldn't have said. She no longer knew herself since the day she'd discovered the worst of Luca, and then spent the night in his arms, driving him on to excess after excess, knowing that she was leaving in the dawn. She had taunted him with cold, heartless lust, and then something had driven her to pay him back in his own coin.

The woman she had once been could never have done it. The woman she had become could have done nothing else. She had told him, in his own terms, that she would not let herself be his victim. After that there was nothing to say.

She supposed he hated her now, which was probably a good thing. At last they could really be free of each other.

She discovered that anger was the best defence against grief, and now that she was alone her anger flared fiercely. He had deceived her in the worst way, creating an illusion for his own purposes. And all the time he'd sat above the scene like some infernal creator, pulling strings. The calculating look she had seen in his eyes had been the true one.

She could not forgive him, not merely because he'd manipulated her, but because he had destroyed her memories.

She knew now why she had never used the word love about their new relationship. It had been hard, shiny, superficial, and, for all its pleasure, unsatisfying. It had ended as it had deserved to end.

Once they had had so much more, and now she blamed herself for being content with so little from a man who had nothing else to give.

And nor did I, she thought. It's too late for me too.

She headed for Europe—France, Switzerland, Italy—visiting out-of-the-way places, while the weeks passed and the days ran into each other. And all the time she knew that if she was to make a final break with the past there was one place that she must go.

She travelled everywhere by train and bus, refusing to hire a car for fear of leaving traces that Luca might pick up if he was pursuing her. She had taken some precautions to prevent herself being found, but she was still being careful. When she went to Carenna it was on an ancient bus that choked and grumbled over the roads.

The sight of the hospital evoked no memories, although it looked as though it had been standing for a hundred years, save for some building work at the rear.

There was the police station, also old, and presumably the same one where Luca had been held to keep him from her. And there was the little church where they were to have been married. Probably the priest was the same man.

But when she wandered in she discovered a young man who had been there only a year. After the first impulse to leave she found herself talking to him. He was easy to talk to, and the whole story came out.

It was two hours before she left, and then she wandered around the town for an hour, trying to come to terms with what she had just learned, and what she had seen. It changed everything. Nothing in the world looked the same in the light of the discovery she had made. But she had nobody with whom to share it.

When her inner haze cleared she found she was standing in front of the little house where she had once lived, for a brief, happy time. It was occupied now by a large family, some of whom she could see through the open door.

She walked closer, noticing automatically that the wallpaper was the same that Luca had put up fifteen years ago. There were rows of leaves of yellow and green.

Suddenly the rows began to swim together. She leaned against the wall, telling herself it would pass soon, but she knew better.

A large woman came out of the house, volubly expressing sympathy, and almost hauling her indoors.

'I was the same with every one of mine,' she said. 'Have you known long?'

'Suspected,' Rebecca said, sipping a hot lemon drink thankfully. 'I haven't been sure until now.'

'And your man? What does he want?'

'A son,' she murmured. 'His heart is set on it.'

'Best you tell him soon.'

She insisted on coming with Rebecca to the bus stop and seeing her safely on board.

'You tell him quick,' she called, waving her off. 'Make him happy.'

Oh, yes, she thought. He would be happy, but she would simply have fallen into his trap. She would not let that happen.

But what else could happen instead, she had no idea.

It was like standing in the centre of a compass, with the needle flickering in all directions, with nowhere to go because everywhere was equally confusing.

At last she recognised that there was only one place where she could do what was necessary. Anger might stifle misery, but it could not deny it altogether. She needed somewhere to grieve for her dead love, and finally bury it. So she set off in that direction.

Luca had said that when you wanted to find somebody you put it in the hands of professionals, but this time the professionals failed him.

Four separate firms, working for three months, had learned only that Rebecca Hanley had travelled to France by ferry. After that she had vanished, and no amount of searching French files produced results. At last he understood that if she had managed to elude such skilled pursuers it meant that her decision to leave him was irrevocable.

When he'd faced that fact, he called them off.

He was back in Rome now, throwing all of himself into maximising Raditore's potential.

'You mean making more money?' Sonia said when he used the phrase. She would never let him get away with corporate-speak.

'Yes, I mean making money,' he said. 'Let's get on with it.'

But he spoke with none of the old bite and that alarmed her more than anything. She could cope with Luca when he was wild, furious, ruthless and rude. But Luca, subdued, was alarming because so unheard-of.

'Go away,' she said to him at last. 'Go right away, not like when you were in London and we talked about business on the phone every night. You're useless to yourself and everyone else while you're here.'

He took her advice and headed his car north, through Assisi, Siena, San Marino. The weather was turning cooler, and driving was pleasant, but everywhere looked the same to him.

Reaching Tuscany, he called in at the construction firm that he'd set up with Frank Solway's money, and from which everything else had grown. It was still flourishing under the command of a good manager that he'd put in charge long ago. Luca examined the accounts, checked the healthy order book, commended his manager on an excellent job, and departed, realising that nobody there needed him.

After that he headed for the place he guessed he'd always meant to go eventually.

There was the long track, stretching up the gentle

slope of the hill. There were the trees from behind which he'd heard angry voices, and had burst through to find a young girl being confronted by three men. The ground was bumpy here, threatening the suspension of his expensive car, but he didn't even notice. His head was too full of visions that blurred and sharpened, taunting him with his sudden reluctance to go further.

He forced himself on until the cottage came into view. He came to a halt near the front door, got out and stood for a moment, surveying the wreckage of what had once been a liveable home. Much of the roof had been burned until it had fallen in, and beams showed against the sky.

A wall was half gone, revealing an interior that had been a bedroom, although there was nothing left to show that now. What remained was black with smoke. Once it had all looked worse. Now the devastation was partly hidden by an overgrowth of weeds. They covered the blackened walls and crowded around the door.

But then Luca saw something that made him stop. The weeds had been partly pruned back, the sharp cuts showing that it had been recently done. And now he could hear faint noises coming from the inside.

Anger possessed him that anyone should dare invade the place that was private to himself. He walked slowly around the cottage, and at the back he saw a tricycle with a makeshift trailer attached to the rear that was little more than a box on wheels. Close inspection revealed that this was indeed how it had started life. It also bore signs of having once fallen to pieces and been inexpertly mended.

Returning to the front, he shouted, 'Come out! What are you doing in there? Come out at once, do you hear me?'

Nothing happened at first. The noise within ceased, as though whoever was there was considering what best to do.

'Come out!' he yelled again. 'Or I'll come in and get you.'

He heard footsteps, then a shadow fell across the door, and a figure emerged into the light.

At first he stared, not believing that she was really there.

He had feared never to see her again, had dreamed of her and found her gone with the first waking moment.

Their last meeting had been three months ago when she had dazzled him with the night of his life, before abandoning him in a gesture of contempt. Now it was like encountering a ghost.

She was dressed in trousers and a tweed jacket, with one hand at her throat to close it against the autumn chill. Her glamorous long hair was gone, cut boyishly short, and returned to its natural light brown colour. Her face was pale, thinner, and there were shadows under her eyes, but she was composed.

She stood only just outside the door as though reluctant to come further out into a world she didn't trust. He approached her slowly. For once he was unsure of himself.

'Are you all right?' he asked.

She nodded.

'What are you doing here, in this rough place?'

'It's peaceful,' she answered. 'Nobody comes calling.'

'How long have you been here?'

'Um—I'm not sure. A week or two, maybe.'

'But—why?'

'Why did *you* come?' she countered.

'Because it's peaceful,' he echoed. 'At least, it is if there are no intruders.'

She nodded. 'Yes,' she said with a faint smile. 'Yes.'

'How are you managing to live here? It's not habitable.'

'It is if you're careful. The stove still works.'

He followed her inside and looked around the kitchen in surprise at how she had made the place liveable.

Everything had been thoroughly cleaned, not an easy task with no electricity. How long, he wondered, had it taken her to sweep up the dust, then scrub the floor and the walls? The range looked as though it had been recently black-leaded.

Warmth was pouring from it now, and a kettle on the top was just beginning to sing. She indicated for him to sit down, and made the tea.

'I know you like sugar,' she said politely, 'but I'm afraid I don't have any. I wasn't expecting visitors.'

'Do you never see anyone?'

'Nobody knows I'm here, not for certain. I ride the bike into the village, put supplies in the trailer, then get back here as quickly as I can, and park it out of sight. Nobody bothers me.'

'You're very determined to hide away. Why? What are you afraid of?'

She seemed surprised by the question.

'Nothing, except being disturbed. I like being alone.'

'Here?'

A faint smile touched her face. 'Do you know of a better place to be alone?'

After a moment he shook his head.

They drank their tea in silence. Luca wanted to say more, but he was nervous and uncertain how to speak to her. This woman, living a hand-to-mouth existence in a ruined shack, had somehow gained the upper hand. He wasn't sure how it had happened, except that she seemed to have discovered a peace that eluded him.

'Do you mind if I look around?' he asked.

'Of course. It's your property.'

'I'm not using that as an excuse to pry. I'm just interested in what you've done.'

There wasn't much to see. Apart from the kitchen only the bedroom was habitable, and that only because the weather was dry. She had pulled the bed away from the hole in the roof and hung a blanket across a rope to make a kind of wall between herself and the exposed part of the room.

One corner of the bed had been badly burned, so that the wooden leg was weakened, and was now boosted by a wooden box. The bed itself sported a patchwork quilt that he remembered from his childhood, although not so bright.

'I hope you don't mind,' she said. 'I found it in a cupboard and when I'd washed the smoke out it looked good.'

'No, I don't mind. My mother made it. But it seems to be all you have on the bed.'

'I've got a cushion for the pillow, and I just huddle up. It's cosy, and I'm warm enough.'

'You are now, but the weather's turning.'

'I like it,' she said stubbornly.

He opened his mouth to protest, but then it struck him that she was right. The place was homely and snug, and although it wasn't actually warm it gave the impression of warmth. He thought of the Allingham with its perfect temperature control, and he could remember only desolation.

'Well, if you like it, that's what counts,' he said, and went back into the kitchen.

'Is this all the food you have?' he asked, opening a cupboard. 'Instant coffee?'

His scandalised tone made her smile briefly.

'Yes, I'm afraid it is instant,' she said. 'I realise that to an Italian that's a kind of blasphemy.'

'You're a quarter-Italian,' he said severely. 'Your grandmother's spirit should rise up and reproach you.'

'She does, but she gets drowned out by the rest of me. I don't keep all my food in here. Fresh vegetables are stored outside, where it's cooler.'

He remembered that outside, attached to the wall, was a small cupboard, made of brick, except for the wooden door. This too had been scrubbed out, and fresh newspaper laid on the shelves, where there was an array of vegetables.

'No meat?' he asked.

'I'd have to keep going into the village to buy it fresh.'

He grunted something, and went back inside.

She poured him another cup of tea, which he drank appreciatively.

'This is good,' he said. 'And it doesn't taste of soot. Whenever I've been here and made coffee, I've always ended up regretting it.'

'Have you returned very often?' she asked.

'Now and then. I come back and cut the weeds, but they've always grown again by the next time.'

'I wonder why you haven't rebuilt it.'

He made a vague gesture. 'I kept meaning to.'

'Why did you come here today?'

He shrugged. 'I was in the area. I didn't know you were here, if that's what you mean.'

It would have been natural, then, to ask her why she'd taken refuge in this spot, when there were so many more comfortable places, but for some reason he was over-come with awkwardness, and concentrated on his tea.

'You've done wonders here,' he said at last, 'but it's still very rough. If anything happened, who could help you?'

She shrugged. 'I'm content.'

'Just the same, I don't like you being here alone. It's better if you...'

He stopped. She was looking at him, and he had the dismaying sense that her face had closed against him. It was like moving through a nightmare. He had been here before.

'I'm only concerned for you,' he said abruptly.

'Thank you, but there's no need,' she said politely. 'Luca, do you want me to leave? I realise that it's your house.'

He shot her a look of reproach.

'You know you don't have to ask me that,' he said. 'It's yours for as long as you want.'

'Thank you.'

He walked outside and strode around to where the bike and trailer were parked.

'Is that thing of real use?' he demanded.

'Oh, yes, if I persevere.' She smiled unexpectedly. 'And I couldn't bring the wood for the range up in a car.'

'You'll be needing some more soon,' he observed, looking at the small pile by the wall. Then he said hast-ily, 'I'll be going now. Goodbye.'

He walked away and got into his car without another word. A brief gesture of farewell, and he was gone. Rebecca stood watching him until the car had vanished.

CHAPTER NINE

SHE tried to sort out her feelings. It had been a shock to see Luca, even though the sound of his voice, calling from outside the cottage, had half prepared her. He had looked nothing like she'd expected. He was thinner, and instead of anger there had been confusion in his eyes. It had been hard, at that moment, to remember that they were enemies.

And, after all, what was there to say? They were civilised people. She could not have said 'You used me, deceived me, and tried to trick me into having your child'. And he could not have said 'You made a fool of me with a pretence of love that was really a display of power'.

They could not have said these things, but the words had been there between them, in the stunned silence.

Their meeting had been less of a strain than it might have been. He had asked no awkward or intrusive questions, and, except for one moment, had not disturbed her tranquillity.

She told herself that she was glad to see him go, but the cottage looked lonely without him. It was his personality, of course, so big that it filled the place and left an emptiness when he departed. When he had been gone for a while the sensation would cease.

She shivered a little and pulled her jacket around her. The weather had cooled rapidly and the place was rather less snug than she had claimed. The last few evenings

she had stayed up late because the kitchen, with the
range, was the only warm room in the house. She had
tried leaving the door to the bedroom open, but the heat
went straight through the open roof.

She began to prepare some vegetables for her evening
meal. When she'd finished she realised that she was running low on water, and took a jug out into the yard, to
the pump. She hated this part because the pump was old
and stiff, and needed all her strength. But the water it
gave was sweet and pure.

She was just about to press down on the handle when
she saw that a car was approaching in the distance. After
a moment she realised that it was Luca, returning.

Setting down the jug, she watched as the car came up
the track until it reached the cottage. Luca got out, nodded to her briefly, and began hauling something from
the back seat that he then carried into the cottage.
Following, Rebecca saw him go right through to the bedroom, and dump a load of parcels on the bed.

He seemed to have raided the village for sheets, blankets and pillows.

'I shall only be here a moment and then I'm going,'
he said brusquely before she could speak.

He headed back to the car at once, delving inside
again and emerging with a cardboard box, which he
brought in and set on the table. This time the contents
were food, fresh vegetables but also tins.

'Luca—'

'That's it,' he said, and hurried through the front door.

But instead of getting into the car he went to the pump
and began to work it vigorously, making the water pour
out into the jug.

'One jug won't last long,' he said tersely. 'Better fetch any other container you've got.'

She fetched two more jugs and when he had filled those too he carried them inside.

'Luca—'

'I just don't want you on my conscience,' he said hurriedly. Then, as she opened her mouth, with a touch of desperation, 'Be quiet!'

Silence.

'Can I say thank you?' she asked at last.

'No need,' he snapped and walked out before she had time to say more.

Through the car window he grunted something that might have been a goodbye, and in another moment she could see his tail lights growing smaller. Then he was gone altogether.

In the bedroom she began to go through the pile of bed linen and realised that there was enough here to ward off the night chills. None of it was very expensive, nothing to overwhelm her, just the gift of a thoughtful friend, if she wanted to take it that way.

But then she remembered the box of food, and something made her hurry back to the kitchen to begin turning it out and examining the contents.

When she did not find what she was looking for her search became feverish, though whether she was trying to prove him better or worse than her suspicions she could not have said.

There were several cartons of fresh milk, for which she was genuinely thankful, tea, a box of shortbread biscuits, fresh bread, butter, ham, eggs and several tins of fruit. And two large, juicy steaks.

But no sugar.

No real, fresh coffee.

Either of those things would have told her that he intended to return. Their absence left her not knowing what to think.

She cooked one of the steaks that evening, and ate it with bread and butter, washed down with a large mug of tea.

She made up the bed, not sorry to exchange the rough sheets for the smooth new ones and pile on the blankets, although she replaced the brightly coloured quilt on top.

Before retiring she treated herself to fresh tea and shortbread, then slipped blissfully between the sheets. She had expected to lie awake for a long time, puzzling about Luca's sudden appearance, but she fell asleep almost at once, and slept soundly for eight hours.

In the morning she felt more refreshed than she had for months. She had been planning to go into the village to stock up, but Luca's gift had made this unnecessary. She could keep her privacy a little longer, and spend today enjoying her favourite occupation, reading one of the books she had brought with her.

She wondered if she ought to do some thorough housework first, in case he returned. She didn't want him to feel that she was neglecting his property.

So she cleared everything away, swept the floor and did a thorough dusting. But still she did not hear his car approaching, and the house began to feel very quiet.

There was a patch of grass in the garden that caught the sun well, and where she could place her chair and read to her heart's content. It also had the advantage that she could not see the track up which he would come, if he came.

It was as well to be free of that kind of temptation, so she chose this spot. After a while, she moved.

When she did finally see a vehicle it was not Luca's expensive car, but an old van that lurched drunkenly along the rough track, until it came to a standstill just outside the gap in the fence that served as a gate. Luca's head appeared through the cab window.

'Have I got room?' he yelled to her.

She studied the gap. 'I don't think so.'

He jumped down and came to see for himself.

'No, it's too narrow by six inches. OK, I'll put that right.'

He went to the back of the van and returned with a large hammer, which he swung at the wood until it gave way. He was dressed in jeans and a shirt, and looked like a different man from the one she had known recently.

One hefty kick completed the demolition of the wood, enabling him to bring the van further in and halt near the front door. He jumped down and looked up into the sky, then at his watch.

'I've got time to make a start, anyway,' he said.

'A start on what?'

But he'd already gone to the back, opening the doors. Inside was a mountain of long planks, and a ladder, which he pulled out and carried around the side of the house, setting it against the wall, just below the hole in the roof.

With Rebecca watching, he climbed up and inspected the damage with the eye of a professional. She saw him tap some beams and try to shake them. What he found seemed to satisfy him, for he shinned back down the ladder.

'A cup of tea would be nice,' he said.

He spoke hopefully but he wasn't looking at her, and she knew that what she said next was crucial. It would take only a word to wither him with the snub she sensed that he dreaded, or to set their relationship on a new, less stressful footing. The future would be decided in this moment.

'Tea already?' she said, smiling slightly. 'You've only just arrived.'

'But the British always give their workmen tea,' he pointed out. 'Otherwise no work ever gets done.'

'In that case, I'll put the kettle on,' she said lightly.

It was done. For good or ill, she had made it possible for him to stay.

While she made the tea she heard him crawling about on the roof, until he descended, went to the van, and came back with a smaller ladder that he took through to the bedroom.

She knew he would check to see if she'd used the sheets and blankets he had brought her, and was glad, now, that she had. A few moments later she found him in there, examining the roof from the inside.

'Those beams won't stand any weight,' he said. 'I'm going to have to take them down, so for a while you'll have less roof than you have now.'

'It hardly makes any difference,' she pointed out cheerfully. 'A large hole or a very large hole, the effect is the same.'

'True. I'm glad to see that you have the right pioneering spirit.'

'Meaning that I'm going to need it? All right, I'm prepared for the worst.'

'You're lucky something hasn't fallen on you already. Look just there.' He was pointing upwards.

'Let me get closer.'

'All right.' He held the ladder while she climbed up, and she could see at once what he meant. The beams were less sturdy than they looked from below, and would not have survived much longer.

'Come down,' he said, 'and I'll get rid of them.'

'Will they land on the bed?' she asked.

'Some of them, yes.'

'Then give me a moment to cover it.'

He helped her protect the bed with the old blankets, then said, 'Right. Stand well clear.'

He was giving orders again, but it did not irk her as it had done before, because here his expertise justified him, and there was reason in everything he did.

Nor did she feel like getting too close when he started swinging the hammer and sending wood crashing down. Some fell outside the house, but some landed inside. Having made an appalling noise, he studied the result with satisfaction and began clearing up the wood.

He performed this task with brisk efficiency, without seeming to notice that this was her bedroom. His only comment came when she tried to lift a heavy plank.

'If you do that, what am I for?' he asked, sounding pained.

She stood back, and waited until all the wood was gone. But then she insisted on helping him gather up the blankets with their burden of dirt and splinters. Together they carried them outside and shook them thoroughly, resulting in a double coughing fit.

'Now we both look a mess,' he said, trying to brush dust out of his hair and from his clothes. 'I need to go into the village, and I think I'll go now before I get any dirtier. Do you want anything?'

She hesitated only a moment before saying, 'Yes, please. I'd like some sugar, and some good coffee.'

It was acceptance, the sign that she was making a small space for him. She wondered how he would react.

'Fine,' he said briefly. 'Nothing else?'

'No, thank you. Nothing else.'

He jumped into the van and made a noisy departure. He was gone an hour and when he returned he had more provisions. There was food, milk, meat and pasta, and the back was piled high with logs, each about twelve inches long.

'For the range,' he said. 'You're going to run out of them soon.'

She had been planning to go to the village for more logs, but it was a heavy job, and her bouts of queasiness had left her not feeling up to it.

She wondered if he suspected, but it was too soon for her to show. And Luca was not perceptive enough to guess.

But when she tried to pick up some logs he stopped her instantly.

'Why don't you take that?' he said, pointing to the box of food. 'I could do with some pasta. You'll find vegetables, tomato purée, and Parmesan cheese.'

It meant nothing. Of course he wanted to do all the heavy work because his pride was tied up in this. And he had always been chivalrous, she recalled. How he had loved to wait on her and tend her, as though she was almost too precious to touch. How gently he had spoken to her, never raising his voice, trying to stand protectively between her and the world.

It was old-fashioned and definitely not 'liberated'. She was a modern, independent woman, who needed no such cosseting. But her eyes softened as she recalled how wonderful it had been.

'Hey!' yelled Luca.

She came out of her happy dream. 'Did you speak to me?'

'Yes. I said, are you going to make that pasta, or are you going to stand there dreaming all day? There's one very hungry man here. Get moving!'

To his bafflement she began to laugh. She tried to stop but something had overtaken her and it quickly became uncontrollable.

'Becky—'

'I'm sorry, I'm trying to—to—'

'What's so funny?' he demanded, aggrieved.

'It's just the contrast—never mind. It's not important.'

'If it's not important, what's stopping you feeding me before I die of hunger?'

'Nothing. I'm on to it now.'

She grabbed the box and hurried inside, still laughing. It took a moment to bring herself under control, but she felt better afterwards. Somehow the little incident had restored her sense of proportion, and she had a feeling it had needed restoring.

Her pasta skills had been rusty when she'd first arrived here, but she'd been polishing them up, and now made a respectable job of it, including the tomato sauce.

'Ready in ten minutes,' she called.

He looked in through the window.

'Fine, I'll just clean up a bit. The logs have made me dirty again.'

She gave the pasta another stir before going outside,

where he was at the pump. He'd stripped off his shirt
and was trying to pump water over himself with one
hand and wash himself with the other. Since the pump
belched water only jerkily, he wasn't managing very
well.

Fetching a few useful items from the kitchen, she went
to help him.

'I'll do the pump,' she said, handing him the soap.

He soaped himself thankfully while she poured water
over him. The sun glinted gloriously off every drop
streaming from the spout, over his long back and powerful arms.

'Now your hair,' she said, spraying something over
the dust that seemed embedded in his scalp, and mas-
saging hard to work up a lather.

'It's in my eyes,' he bellowed.

'Oh, stop being such a baby!'

'You're a heartless woman.'

'OK, here comes the rinse,' she cried, pumping again.

When the suds had gone she handed him the towel
she'd brought out and he dried himself thankfully.

'That's better. Hey, what's this?' He snatched up a
plastic cylinder from the bench where she'd set it.
'Washing-up liquid?'

'It's as good as anything for the purpose.'

'You washed my hair with washing-up liquid?' he repeated, aghast. 'Do you realise you've made me smell
of lemon?'

'Well, I had to use something before your hair set
solid, and the only shampoo I have smells of perfume.'

'Lemon's just fine,' he said hastily.

Now that the ice had been broken they bickered amiably over the meal, inching their way carefully towards a place where this new relationship would be possible.

After lunch he went around the house, testing locks, and was shocked by what he found.

'The front door doesn't lock properly, and the back door doesn't lock at all. Lucky I brought some more.'

As he fixed the new locks into place he said crossly, 'You've been sleeping here like this? No locks? Anyone could have walked in.'

'Since nobody comes here, it didn't seem important. Still, I'm glad you've done that.'

He went back to work on the roof, hauling wood up and hammering mightily, until he had put in place a rough frame.

'With any luck, this will be your last night under that hole,' he said, looking up from directly beneath it. 'By tomorrow night I should have rigged up some covering.'

'It's going to be very cosy in here,' she said appreciatively. 'Thank you, Luca.'

But he was yawning and didn't seem to hear her.

'I feel as though I'm falling apart,' he said, rubbing his shoulders as he wandered out into the kitchen.

'Let's eat.'

He collected logs to refill the range while she lit candles, for the light was fading fast.

A candlelit meal might have been romantic, but he seemed determined to rob the atmosphere of any semblance of romance, watching her cooking like a hawk and making a stream of interfering suggestions until at last she said crossly, 'All right, do it yourself.'

'I will. I will.'

'Fine!'

'Fine!'

She went into the bedroom and sat on the bed, in a huff, for about ten minutes. Then she returned to the kitchen, having recovered her sense of humour.

'You'll turn the food sour,' he objected.

'No, I'm all right now. Shall I take over?'

'No, thank you,' he said with more haste than politeness. 'I have everything under control. This will take a while, so why don't we have mushrooms and rice first? You can prepare the mushrooms and I'll put the water on for the rice.'

She worked on the mushrooms for the next few minutes, until forced to stop by a queasy stomach.

'Are you all right?' Luca asked.

'There's just something about the smell of raw mushrooms,' she said.

'You've never said that before.'

'I'm saying it now,' she said fretfully.

'It'll be all right when they're cooked.'

'Now you're talking.'

She went out for some fresh air, wanting to escape his notice. The nausea was there again but a few deep breaths took care of it. If last time was anything to go by, she should be coming to the end of her sickness. If only Luca did not suspect the truth before then.

As for what she would tell him, she was so confused that even thinking about it would be a waste of time. Before he came here she'd had no intention of informing Luca that she was carrying his child. Now? She didn't know. But, for the moment, she intended to keep the decision in her own hands.

She knew, though, that time was running out. If she did not tell him, she would have to leave soon and decide where to have her baby.

When she went back inside she was smiling. He was busy cooking the mushrooms and rice, and somehow after that he ended up cooking the whole meal.

'You're a great cook,' she said as they ate.

'That's not what you used to say. You used to criticise my cooking.'

'Only because I was jealous. You were better than me. It made me so mad.'

He stared. 'And I thought I'd never get you to admit that.'

'You knew all the time, huh?'

'Of course. There was never anything wrong with my cooking.'

'You arrogant so-and-so.'

'Well, there wasn't. I'm a great cook. Why not be honest about it?'

'Not only arrogant, but conceited.'

'Always was,' he said briefly. 'Do you want those extra mushrooms?'

She gave him her last mushroom, and the subject was allowed to die.

The candles were burning down as he helped her with the washing-up. Then he said, 'That's it for today. I'm ready to turn in. Goodnight, Becky.'

He gave her a brief nod and walked outside. She went to the door, expecting to see him get into the cab and drive away, but instead he went to the back and climbed in. When he did not reappear she went to look for him, and found him unwrapping a bed roll by the light of a torch.

'What are you doing?' she asked.

'Going to bed.'

'Out here?'

'Where else?'

'Haven't you got a nice, comfortable hotel room?'

'Yes, but it's several miles away, and I'm not leaving you here alone. It's too isolated.'

'Luca—'

'Goodnight. And, Becky—'

'Yes?'

'Lock the front door.'

'I thought you were going to fend off invaders for me.'

'I meant, lock it against me.'

'Do you plan to come into the house?'

'No.'

'Then I don't need to lock it. Anyway, there's a big hole in the roof, in case you hadn't noticed.'

'Becky, will you quit arguing and just lock the door?'

'All right, all right.' She went away, muttering, 'But it seems silly to me.'

As she snuggled down in her own bed she reflected how odd it was that she should feel so able to trust his word. He had said he would not intrude on her, and she knew that he would not.

She was up early next morning, but he was already moving about outside. She opened the door, calling, 'Coffee!' and he hurried in, moving stiffly, like a man who'd spent a cold night on a hard floor.

As he drank his coffee she heated up some washing water for him, then cooked bacon and eggs while he washed. He said little over breakfast, being absorbed in the food, and as soon as he'd finished he went straight to work.

Halfway through the morning she took him a snack, and they drank tea together.

'You're doing a lovely job,' she said, indicating the roof, which was taking shape.

'I got my start this way: hammering my own nails in and hiring as little help as I could manage with. I could turn my hand to anything in those days, but it's years since I did any honest work.'

He grinned suddenly. 'It's also years since I got as filthy as this.' He spread out his hands with their finely manicured nails, looking incongruous with the grazes they had acquired in the last two days.

'I bet you weren't hammering your own nails in for long,' she said.

'I employed a few men and it went to my head; I took on more than we could cope with and ended up having to work my head off at night, on my own. I snatched one job right out from under the nose of the biggest builder in the district. He thought the really profitable jobs were his by rights, and he didn't like it. That's how I got this.' He rubbed his scar.

'You had a fight?'

'No, but for a while I was pretty sure he was going to send his gang for me. I took to spending my nights in the yard, staying awake, waiting for them.'

'And they came for you?'

'No, they never did. But I got so tired that I fell off a ladder.' He grinned in rueful self-mockery.

'You're kidding me.'

'No, really. Mind you, I always let people believe it was done in a fight. My stock went up no end.'

'How did you get from being a builder to being where you are now?'

'I bought some land to build on. It increased in value and suddenly I was a speculator. It's more profitable to buy and sell houses than to build them, so I concentrated on that. Once I started making money I couldn't stop. In fact, it's not difficult to make more money than you could ever need if you devote yourself to it twenty-four hours a day, and never think of anything else.'

'You must have thought about something else at some time,' she said. 'What about your wife?'

'Drusilla married me for my money.'

'What did you marry for?'

He was silent awhile before he said, 'She was a status symbol. Her family have a very old title, and only a few years earlier she wouldn't have looked at me. That made me feel good.'

He grimaced. 'Not nice, is it? But I'm not a nice man, Becky. I never really was. You made me better, but without your influence I reverted to being what I am.'

'No!' she said violently. 'That's too easy, too glib.'

'It's the truth about me. And it's not so long ago that you'd have been the first to say so. If I can face it now, why can't you?'

'Because I don't believe it *is* the truth. Nobody can be explained that simply. Luca, are you trying to make me feel that it's my fault, that I let you down in some way?'

'No, I'm not. I'm saying that you can't buck nature.'

'What nature? Who knows what anybody's nature is? It isn't fixed, it develops through what happens to you.'

'It's sweet of you to defend me—'

'I'm not defending you,' she said crossly, 'I'm calling you a lame-brained idiot.'

'I'm just saying that I know myself—'

'Rubbish. Nobody knows themselves that well.'

'That time in Carenna, when all I could think of was

taking care of you—I never acted meek and mild with anyone else before, and I've never done it since.'

'You never had a baby with anyone else.'

'That's true,' he said quietly.

Carried away by her arguments, she'd failed to see the pit opening at her feet until she fell into it. She had forgotten about the cause of their quarrel. Now it came back to her, and she fell silent.

'Do you want to talk about that?' he asked.

'Not really,' she said hastily. 'There's nothing to say.'

'No.' He seemed deflated. 'No, I guess there isn't.'

CHAPTER TEN

SHE was gathering up the remains of the snack and preparing to go indoors when she heard the faint sound of a voice behind her.

'I'm sorry, Becky, for everything.'

'What?'

She turned sharply, not sure if she'd really heard the words, but Luca was already rising.

'Time I was getting back to work,' he said, stretching his limbs. 'Let's see how far we can get with this roof today.'

He fixed several beams, but then the light was too poor for him to go any further, so he fetched some roofing felt from the van.

'I'll just nail this over the gap for tonight, so that you'll have some cover,' he said. 'Tomorrow, with any luck, the roof should be finished.'

When he'd fixed the felt into place he ate the meal she'd prepared as quickly as possible. She had hoped they might talk some more, but he said goodnight and left.

He had made the repairs just in time. That night the heavens opened. Summer was finally over and the first storm of autumn was impressive, especially to the woman looking up at the felt, and wondering how strong it was. But no water was dripping down into the bedroom. As a builder, Luca knew his stuff.

Just as she was beginning to relax she heard a crash

from outside, and sat up sharply, listening for any further worrying noises. But the pounding of the rain blotted out all else.

At last she got out of bed, threw on a dressing gown and made her way outside. The wind hit her like a hammer, hard enough to blow her back inside if she hadn't clung to the doorpost. Breathing hard, she steadied herself and tried to look around through the rain that was coming down in sheets.

She could see no sign of trouble, but another noise came from around the corner of the cottage and she headed that way, arriving just as a fork of lightning illuminated the lean-to where the logs were stored, revealing that the roof had come down.

'Oh, great!' she muttered. 'Now the wood will get wet and it won't burn, and the kitchen will fill with smoke, and probably fifty other things will happen. Great! Great! Great!'

There was only one thing to do. Gathering up a pile of logs, she began to stagger back to the front door. On the way the dressing gown fell open and she tripped over the belt, falling into the mud and taking the logs with her.

Cursing furiously, she got to her feet and surveyed the soaking logs, aided by the lightning that obligingly flashed at that moment.

'Damn!' she told the heavens. A blast of thunder drowned her out. 'And the same to you!'

Suddenly Luca's voice came from near by. *'Becky, what are you doing out here?'*

'What does it look as if I'm doing?' she demanded at the top of her voice. 'Dancing the fandango? The lean-to came down and the wood's getting even wetter than I am, which is saying a good deal.'

'OK, I'll fetch it in,' he yelled back. 'Go inside and get dry.'

'Not while there's wood to be moved.'

'I'll do it.'

'It'll take too long for one person. It'll be drenched.'

'I said I'll do it.'

'Luca, I swear if you say that once more I'll brain you.'

He ground his teeth. 'I am only trying to take care of you.'

'*Then don't!* I haven't asked you to. I'll do the wood on my own.'

'You will *not* do it on your own!' He tore his hair. 'While we're arguing, it's getting wet.'

'Then let's get on,' she said through gritted teeth, and went back to the pile of logs before he could argue again.

They got about a quarter of the wood inside before he said, 'That's it. There's enough there for a few days, and during that time we can bring some of the rest in and dry it out.'

'All right,' she said, glad to leave off now her point was made. 'Come in and get yourself dry.'

They squelched back indoors, Luca slamming the van's open door in passing with a force that showed his feelings.

Once inside, Rebecca lit some candles, then rooted inside a cupboard, glad that the one luxury she had allowed herself was a set of top-quality towels and two vast bathrobes. They were chosen to be too big, so that the occupant could snuggle deep inside, which was fortunate, or Luca could never have got into one.

'Why didn't you call me?' he asked, sitting down and pulling the robe as far around him as he could.

'Because I'm not a helpless little woman.'

'Just a thoroughly awkward one,' he grumbled.

'Oh, hush up!' She silenced him by tossing a hand towel over his head and beginning to rub, ignoring the noises that came from underneath.

'What was that?'

He emerged from the towel, tousled and damp, and looking oddly young.

'I said you should have knocked on the van door and woken me.'

'I'm surprised you didn't hear the lean-to go down, the noise it made.'

But then she remembered that he had always slept heavily, sometimes with his head on her breast.

'Well, I didn't. It was mere chance that I woke up when I did. Otherwise, I suppose you'd have taken the whole lot indoors.'

'No, I'd have been sensible and stopped after a few, like we did.'

He grunted.

'And don't grunt like that as though you couldn't believe a word I say.'

'I know you. You'd say anything to win an argument.'

She grinned. 'Yes, I would. So don't take me on.'

'No, I've got the bruises from that, haven't I?' he asked wryly.

'We've both got bruises,' she reminded him. 'Old and recent.'

He looked at her cautiously. 'But you're still speaking to me?'

'No, I'm speaking to this man who turned up to mend

the roof,' she said lightly. 'Good builders are hard to find.'

He gave a brief laugh. 'My only honest skill.'

'Don't be so hard on yourself,' she said quietly.

She thought he might say something, but he only grabbed the towel and began rubbing his head again.

She made some tea and sandwiches and they ate in near silence. He seemed tired and abstracted, and she wondered if he was regretting that he had ever started this.

'What happened to you?' he asked suddenly, while he was drying his feet.

'How do you mean?'

'Where did you vanish to?'

'Didn't your enquiry agents tell you that?'

He grimaced an acknowledgement. 'They traced you to Switzerland, then the trail went cold. I guess you meant it to.'

'Sure. I knew you'd hire the best, and they'd check the airlines and the ferries, and anywhere where there was passport control. So I slipped across the Swiss-Italian border "unofficially".'

He stared. 'How?'

She smiled. 'Never mind.'

'As simple as that?'

'As simple as that. Then I made all my journeys by train or bus, because if I'd hired a car I'd have left a trail.'

'Is that why you have that incredible bike around the back?'

'That's right. I bought it for cash. No questions asked.'

'I should think so. They must have been glad to get

rid of it before it fell apart. What's that thing at the back made of?'

'You mean my trailer?'

'Is that what you call it?'

'Certainly,' she said with dignity. 'I'm very proud of it. I just got some boxes and hammered them together. There was an old pram in the little barn behind the house and I took the wheels off. I'm sorry, I know they belong to you.'

'Don't worry, I won't ask for them back. If it's the pram I think it is, it was collapsing anyway. In fact, it was collapsing when my parents got it. My father won it in a card game when my mother was expecting me, and I gather she made him sorry he was born. I can't believe that you actually use it.'

'I only go short distances to the village for supplies, food, logs, that sort of thing.'

'You've brought logs back in that little box?'

'I did once, but I put in too many and it fell apart. I had to come back here for a hammer and nails, then go back, put it together and finish the job. The logs were just where I'd left them.'

'Of course. People around here are honest. But why didn't you have the logs delivered?'

'Because then people would have known for sure where I lived.'

'What about hotels when you were travelling? Didn't they ask to see your passport?'

She shrugged. 'I pass as Italian. I've been all over the country, never staying anywhere for very long.'

He drew a long breath. 'Of all the wily, conniving...! I thought I was a schemer, but I've got nothing on you.'

'Pretty good, huh?' she said with a touch of smiling cockiness.

'You could teach me a thing or two,' he said, grinning back at her.

But their smiles were forced, and faded almost at once.

'I kept meaning to stop awhile in this place or that,' Rebecca continued, 'but I never felt I belonged in any of them. So I always moved on to the next place.'

'Until you came here.' He left the implication hanging in the air, but she did not pick it up.

At last he said quietly, 'You were very determined to escape me, weren't you?'

'Yes,' she said simply.

He didn't answer, and she looked up to see his face in the flickering candlelight. It might have been the distorting effect of the little flames, but she thought she had never seen such a look of unbearable sadness.

He didn't turn away or try to hide it, just sat regarding her with a look so naked and defenceless that it was as much as she could do not to reach out to him.

'Luca...' She didn't mean to say his name, but it slipped out.

Then emotion overcame her and she covered her eyes, letting her head drop onto her arm on the table. She didn't know what else to do. What she was feeling now was beyond tears: despair for the lost years, the chances that could never be recovered, the love that seemed to have died, leaving behind only desolation.

And if there was a hint of hope, it was of a muted kind. She might yet have his child, but it was too late for them.

She thought she felt a light touch on her hair, and

perhaps her name was murmured very softly, but it was hard to be sure, and she did not look up. She didn't want him to see her tears.

She heard him go to the stove and put in some more logs, then sit down again.

'That will keep it going until morning,' he said. 'Go back to bed and keep warm.'

She looked up to see him near the door.

'Where are you going?'

'Back to the van. I'll put some dry clothes on in there, and let you have the towels back tomorrow.'

'No, wait!'

She hadn't asked herself where he would sleep, but it seemed monstrous for him to have to return to his bleak conditions while she had all the comfort.

'You can't go back to the van,' she said.

'Of course I can. I'm quite happy there.'

She jumped up, arm outstretched to detain him, but stopped abruptly at the weakness that came over her. For a moment her head was fuzzy and the kitchen danced about her. Then the giddiness cleared.

She wasn't sure whether he'd taken hold of her, or whether she was clinging to him, but they were gripping each other tightly and she was furious with herself. Now he would know.

She waited for his exclamation, the questions: why hadn't she told him? And at the end of it all she would feel cornered and trapped.

'Maybe you didn't have enough for supper,' he said. 'Hauling logs about on an empty stomach. Shall I get you something?'

'No, thank you,' she said slowly.

'Then you should go straight back to bed. Come on.'

He kept a firm but impersonal hold on her all the way into the bedroom, held her while she sat down on the bed, then tucked her in.

'All right?'

'Yes. Thank you, Luca.'

'Let's get some sleep for what's left of the night. There's another heavy day tomorrow.'

He closed the door quietly behind him, and after a moment she heard the front door also close.

The darkness held no answers. She tried to conjure up his eyes in that brief moment when he'd steadied her, and to read what she had seen there.

But she had seen only what he'd chosen to reveal. Nothing. His eyes had been blank, their depths barred to her. It was as though he'd stepped back, giving her space, even space enough for a denial, if she wished.

She had thought she knew him through and through. Now she wondered if she had ever known the first thing about him.

She discovered in the following days that the space she'd sensed him offering her was no illusion. In a way it was what he'd done since the moment he appeared, sleeping outside in all weathers, never intruding or saying a word that could have come from a lover.

But now something was different, as though he too needed that space. Perhaps, she thought, he was doing this for himself. He would finish the house to keep her safe, but then he would drive away and never ask about the child. Because now he did not want to know. It was rather like living with a ghost. But above all it was peaceful, and peace was what she most valued.

Bit by bit the house was coming alive again. The completion of the roof would mean that another room, which had been completely open to the skies, would become inhabitable. Rebecca set herself to clean it out, sweeping soot from the floor and the walls.

Luca's response was to vanish for nearly a day. When he returned he had a small portable generator and a vacuum cleaner.

'I had to go to Florence to get these,' he said. 'The generator was the last they had. It's not really big enough, but the bigger one had just been bought by someone else, and all my pleading wouldn't make him part with it. Still, it's big enough to scoop up the soot, and prevent you looking like a chimney sweep.'

She blew a stray lock of hair away from her forehead, but it settled back again. He grinned and brushed it back.

'Is supper ready?'

'Nope. I didn't know if you were coming back, so I didn't prepare anything.'

'OK. That's cool.'

'Oh, stop being nice!' she growled. 'It's steak. I'll start it now.'

From then on the job was easier and they had some light in the evenings, although they still relied on the range for warmth and cooking.

'You could move in there,' Rebecca said cautiously one day, when the room was finished. 'To sleep, I mean. Better than the van.'

He considered for a moment. 'OK,' he said at last briefly.

He took the van into the village and returned with an iron bedstead, bought second-hand, as he explained to her with great pride.

'It's very narrow,' she said doubtfully. 'It can't be more than two feet six.'

'People live in small houses around these parts. The furniture has to be narrow.'

But the mattress was unusable, and he was forced to buy another. This time he splashed out on a brand-new mattress that was a foot wider than the bed.

'You see, it won't matter that the bed is narrow,' he said triumphantly. 'All I'll feel is the mattress beneath me.'

'But it'll hang over six inches each side. Every time you turn over you'll roll off.'

'Nonsense. I've worked it out scientifically.'

He explained the science of it to her in detail, and Rebecca made a noise indicating scorn. That night he went scientifically to bed and fell out scientifically three times. After that he put the mattress on the floor and used the bed as a dumping ground for anything he couldn't find a place for.

Humour was a lifeline, making the journey possible until they knew where the road led. But even while they were laughing over his mishaps they knew that the fragile atmosphere could not last forever.

The thing that shattered it crept up on them without warning. They were sitting in the kitchen, listening to a concert on Rebecca's battery radio, and laughing over Luca's attempts to repair the 'trailer'.

'Well, I've got it together,' he said at last, 'but is it worth it? Do you have a use for it?'

She shook her head.

'Good.' He tossed it into a corner, where a wheel fell off.

'My father insisted on keeping that thing,' he said

after a moment, 'just in case they had another child. But
it never happened. Then Mama died when I was ten.'

'Yes, I remember you telling me once,' she said,
thinking back. 'It must have been lonely without broth-
ers or sisters.'

'I had my father to look after. He was lost without
her.' He gave a brief laugh. 'Bernardo Montese, the local
giant, big man, made everyone afraid of him. But he
was a softie inside, so first she looked after him, then I
did. It was like looking after a child.'

'You loved him very much, didn't you?' she asked
softly.

'Yes, I did. We were on the same wavelength. I realise
now that it was partly because he was like a child that
never grew up. You wouldn't have thought it to look at
him shouting the odds, but under all that mountainous
strength there was a hidden weakness, and if you
touched it he crumbled.'

She watched him, holding her breath, knowing that
something was happening. Beneath the calm of that little
cottage things were whirling out of control. If she
wanted to stop it happening she must do it now.

'Go on,' she whispered.

'And he still wouldn't get rid of the pram. He said
my wife would be glad of it one day. I didn't have the
heart to tell him it was only fit for the scrap heap. The
thought seemed to mean a lot to him. Then he got drunk
and fell into a stone quarry, and died the next day. I was
sixteen.'

He had talked about his parents when they knew each
other before, but never like this. She tried to find the
right words to encourage him to say more, but before
she could speak he said,

'When we met in London...' He stopped as though his courage had failed him.

'Go on,' she said.

'I never asked you about the birth. I kept meaning to, but—'

'The time was never right.'

'No, it wasn't. But I'd like to know, if you can bear to speak of it. Was it very hard?'

'It was over fairly quickly. She was small, being premature. It was what came after that was hard. I longed for you so much. I didn't know that you were being kept from me by the police.'

'Your father must have called them while I was calling the ambulance. They arrived fast and arrested me, on his say-so, for ''violent behaviour''. I pleaded to be allowed to go with you, but they wouldn't let me. I remember the ambulance doors shutting, and it driving away with you inside, while I was being pulled in the other direction by the police.

'I went mad, and then I did become violent. It took four of them to haul me away, and I know I gave one of them a bloody nose, so then they had something to charge me with.

'I was in the cells for days, unable to get any news of you. Then your father came to see me. He said the baby had been born dead, so I could ''forget any ideas I had''.'

'He said what?' She was staring at him.

'He said our child was born dead. Becky, what is it?' She was staring at him with a livid look that alarmed him.

'She wasn't born dead,' she whispered. 'She lived just a few hours in an incubator. I saw her. She was so tiny, and attached to machines in all directions. It looked terrible, but I knew the doctors and nurses were fighting for her. They tried so hard, but it was no use. She just slipped away.'

'But she was alive?' he asked hoarsely. 'She actually lived, even if just for a little while?'

'Yes.'

'Were you able to hold her?'

'Not while she was alive. She needed to be in the incubator. It was her only chance. But when she'd died they wrapped her in a shawl and put her in my arms. I kissed her, and told her that her mother and father loved her. And then I said goodbye.'

'You can remember that?'

'Yes, at that stage I was still functioning. The depression didn't hit me until a few hours later.'

'Didn't you wonder where I was?'

'Yes, I kept asking Dad, and he said, "They're still trying to find him."'

'He said *that*, knowing I was trapped in a cell, where he'd put me?' Luca asked with quiet rage.

'He kept saying you'd gone. And then she was dead, and after that—' she faltered '—after that things became dark. A black cloud enveloped me without warning. I felt crushed, suffocated, and absolutely terrified. The whole world seemed to be full of horror, and it went on and on without hope.'

She passed a hand over her eyes. 'Maybe it would have happened anyway, with losing the baby. But maybe if we could have been together it wouldn't have happened. Or I might have got over it sooner. I'll never know.'

'There was nothing your father wouldn't do to separate us,' Luca said. 'No matter how wicked or deceitful, it didn't matter as long as he got his own way.'

She nodded. 'I think he believed it would be easy at the start. Only then things spiralled out of control, and he had to do worse and worse things so as not to have to admit he'd been wrong. He kept trying to rewrite the facts to prove he'd been right, and of course he couldn't do it.'

He looked at her quickly. 'You defend him?'

'No, but I don't think he started out as a bad man. He became one because he didn't know how to say sorry. He destroyed us but he also destroyed himself. He knew what he'd done. He couldn't admit it but he knew, and he couldn't face it.'

'Did you ever confront him with what he'd done?'

'Yes, just once. We had a terrible fight and I told him that he'd killed my baby.'

'What did he say?'

'Nothing. Just stared at me and turned white. Then he walked away. Later I found him staring into space. About a year after that he had a massive heart attack. He was only fifty-four, but he died almost instantly.'

'I am not sorry for him,' Luca said with bitter emphasis. 'I do not forgive him, and I will not pretend that I do.'

'I know. I can pity him a little because I saw what he'd done to himself as well as to us. But forgiveness is more than I can manage too. Besides...'

She was silent for a long moment, getting up and pacing the room as though tormented by indecision.

'What is it?' he asked, looking up at her quickly. 'Is there more?'

'Yes, there's something I've been waiting to tell you,

but it had to be when the moment was right. Now, I think...'

She stopped, torn by indecision, even though she knew there was no turning back. Luca took her hands between his.

'Tell me, Becky,' he said. 'Whatever it is, it's time I knew.'

CHAPTER ELEVEN

'Yes,' she said. 'You ought to know. Luca, have you ever been back to Carenna?'

'No,' he said after a moment.

'Me neither, until recently. I went a few weeks ago, and I found out something else my father lied about.'

She stopped again. Suddenly the next part seemed momentous, and she wondered if she had been wise to start.

'Go on,' he said.

'I'd always thought she died without being baptised, without a name. Dad never told me otherwise.'

'You mean—?'

'She's there, in the churchyard. She was baptised by the hospital chaplain.'

'But how could you not have known?'

'They took her away to the incubator as soon as she was born, while I stayed behind for the nurses to finish tending to me. The chaplain was already in the baby unit, seeing another child. They thought our little girl might only have a few minutes, so he baptised her there and then, in case he wasn't in time.'

'And they never told anybody?'

'Yes, they told Dad. I suppose they assumed he'd tell me, but he never did. But she was buried in consecrated ground.

'The priest died last year, but I spoke to the new one, and it's all there in the records. Apparently the priest held a little funeral, and told Dad when it was going to be. He couldn't tell me, because my father kept him away, and he didn't know where you were. So when our daughter was buried—' a tremor shook her '—none of her family were there.'

'Not even your father?'

'He wanted to pretend that she never existed, and he wanted *me* to forget about her. So he tried to blot her out, and blot you out. He even told the priest her name was Solway.'

'You mean—?'

'That's the name on her grave,' she said with rising anger. 'Rebecca Solway. But she's there, Luca. She didn't vanish into the void. He didn't manage to obliterate her, not completely.'

Luca rose violently and paced the room as though sitting still was suddenly intolerable. He began to shake his head like a beast in pain, and she thought she had never seen a man's face look so ravaged.

At last he came to a halt, and without warning swung his fist into the wall. It landed with a thunderous shock, and immediately he did it again, and then again. It was as well that the old cottage was made of solid stone or it could never have withstood the impact of his rage and agony.

'Oh, God!' he kept saying. 'Dear God! Dear God!'

Torn with pity for him, she put her arms around his body. He didn't stop thumping the wall, but his free hand grasped her so tightly that he almost crushed her.

'Luca—Luca, please...'

She wasn't sure that he heard her. He seemed lost in a haze of misery, where only the rhythmic thumping made sense.

At last he was too tired to go on, and leaned his head

against the stone, shaking with distress. Rebecca rested her own head against his back, weeping for him. She could endure her own pain, but his pain tore her apart.

He turned far enough to draw her against his chest in a convulsive grip.

'Hold on to me,' he said hoarsely, 'or I shall go mad. Hold me, Becky, hold me.'

He almost fell against her. All his massive physical strength seemed to have drained out of him, and there was only hers left to save him.

She did as he asked and held him. The path he was travelling was one she herself had walked only a short time before, and she resolved that he would not walk it alone, as she had done.

Leaning on her, he got back to the chair and almost fell into it. His eyes were vacant, as though fixed on some inner landscape where there was only desolation.

His right hand was red and raw where the wall had torn it, and she gently took hold of it, sensing how even the lightest touch made him wince. She began to dab it with water, her eyes blurred with tears at what he had done to himself in his torment.

She dropped to one knee beside him so that she could clean the bleeding wound. He stared at it, as though wondering how it had happened.

'What did it look like?' he asked at last.

'What, darling?' The word slipped out naturally.

'Her grave, what was it like?'

'Just a little grave, very plain and small, with the name and the date she was born and died.'

'And nobody of her own was there at her funeral,' Luca murmured. This fact in particular seemed to trouble him. 'Poor little thing. Laid away in darkness, all alone.'

He shook his head as though trying to get free of something.

'I was glad when I found out,' Rebecca said. 'It's better than her having no baptism and no proper burial. I thought you'd be glad too.'

'I am glad about that,' he said quickly. 'But we should have been told. If I'd known, I would have gone back there to see her, often. She wouldn't have been alone.'

It was as if a light had shone through her mind, illuminating him as never before. Luca was an Italian, with the Italian's attitude to death. Like almost everything else in Italy, it was a family matter. A child's grave was visited regularly, with flowers and tokens on birthdays, because even in death that child was a member of the family. To him it was an outrage that his daughter had lain unvisited for fifteen years.

'She's still there, waiting for us,' she said. 'Perhaps it's time her parents visited her together.'

He couldn't speak. Dumbly he nodded.

'But you should see a doctor about your hand first.'

He made an impatient movement. 'It's nothing.'

'I've only got water to clean it with, and I'm afraid it will get infected. Or you may have broken something.'

'Nonsense, I'm never hurt.'

'Oh, yes, you are,' she said softly. 'Now, come and lie down.'

After a moment he nodded and let her lead him to his bed. His hand was clearly painful and he had to accept her help to undress down to vest and shorts, but when she mentioned it he said gruffly, 'It'll be all right tomorrow.'

By the next day it was swollen and still hurting him, but he wouldn't consider 'wasting time' with a doctor.

His manner was feverish, as though nothing mattered but getting to Carenna as fast as possible.

'We can't go in that van,' Rebecca observed. 'Where's your car?'

'Garaged in the village, with the man who hired me the van.'

'You'll have to show me how to drive it.'

'I'll drive it.'

But he had to give up after the first mile, and she drove the clanking vehicle the rest of the way.

'Turn left, down there,' he said almost as soon as they were in the village. 'Becky, I said down there.'

'Later,' she said, bringing the van to a noisy halt outside the doctor's surgery. 'First we go in here.'

'I told you I'm all right,' he groaned.

'And I'm telling you that you're not.'

'Becky, I don't want—'

She lost her temper.

'Did I ask you what you want? Luca, it's very simple. I'm the only person who can drive at the moment, and I'm going nowhere until you've been to the doctor.'

'That's blackmail.'

'Yes, it is. So what?'

'You're just being stupid.'

'Fine, then the doctor can tell me so.'

But the doctor said no such thing. He was an old man with modern ideas, who'd equipped his surgery with a lot of good equipment, including a small X-ray machine. It took only a short time to establish that Luca had cracked two bones and smashed a third.

'It's good that you came straight to me, *signore*,' said the doctor as he set the hand in plaster. 'Otherwise your hand would have been crippled. You were very wise.'

He regarded them knowingly. 'Or maybe you are just fortunate in your wife?'

'Yes,' Luca said.

'Here are some painkillers, and two of these other pills will give you a good night. I hope you weren't planning anything strenuous for the rest of today.'

'No,' Rebecca said quickly. 'We were thinking of a journey, but now we've put it off until tomorrow.'

Luca simply nodded. He was looking worn and ill, and she sensed that this was only partly due to his injured hand. It was as though all the fight had gone out of him. He even agreed to stay quietly in the doctor's waiting room while she returned the van and collected the car.

It was dusk as she drew up at the cottage, and she immediately set about getting the place warm and making him comfortable. His appetite was poor but he managed to eat some pasta with his left hand.

'Go to bed now,' she said gently. 'And I think you should take the proper bed, and I'll have the mattress.'

But he shook his head firmly and she made no further protest. He accepted her help undressing, then let her usher him into the rough bed like a mother with an exhausted child. He touched her hand briefly.

'Thank you,' he said. 'For everything.'

She squeezed his hand, kissed him briefly and hurried out.

They were on the road early next morning, eating up the miles to Carenna in the silkily gliding car.

For this journey they had abandoned the jeans and sweaters in which they had been living, becoming sober and conventional again. In a severe, well-cut suit, Luca might have been the man she'd met again months ago,

but he was not that man. His face had changed. It was
thinner and almost haggard, as though he'd aged overnight.

At the start of the journey she touched his hand, and
he briefly smiled at her, but then seemed to withdraw
into a place inside himself. She could only guess at the
suffering that was there.

They reached Carenna in the early afternoon and
drove straight to the church. The town had grown since
they were last there together, the streets were more
crowded, and once they were caught in a traffic jam.

'Do you remember the hospital?' she asked, indicating
the building through the window.

'Yes, I remember.'

They were moving again, turning a corner so that he
could see the builders working at the rear. He followed
it with his eyes until the building was out of sight.

In another few minutes they had reached the little
church, where they had once planned to be married. As
she parked the car Rebecca glanced at Luca, wondering
what he was thinking and feeling. But his set face
showed no reaction and she was slightly disappointed.
Until then she had felt that this was something they were
doing together. Now she began to feel that he was further away than she had suspected, in a place where she
was not invited to follow.

'Is she here?' Luca asked as they entered the churchyard. 'Can you show me where she lies?'

'Yes, come with me.'

The little grave was in a far corner and they had to
pick their way carefully because the graveyard was
densely crowded. At last they reached the little enclosed
section where several children lay together.

'Why are they here and not with their families?' Luca wanted to know.

But then his eyes fell on the sign, *Gli Orfani*. Orphans. She saw him flinch.

At the end of the line they found the tiny grave bearing the legend 'Rebecca Solway', and the date of her birth and death. The stone was no longer quite straight, and although the grass had been cut back neatly the grave still looked as though it was struggling not to vanish among the others.

Luca dropped to one knee, leaning forward and peering at the words. Rebecca knelt beside him and saw how he reached out one big hand and laid it flat on the grass.

'She must have been so tiny,' he said in a choking voice.

'Yes, she was. You could have held her in that hand.'

He closed his eyes. She could feel him trembling and her heart ached for him. She waited for him to turn to her.

The moment stretched on and on. He did not move and his eyes stayed fixed on the stone. At last she got up and walked away.

The little church was empty as she pushed the door open. Everything was quiet and her footsteps sounded very loud. It was disappointing that Father Valetti wasn't here. She had liked the young priest with his round, friendly face and understanding eyes.

She strolled out again and saw Luca coming towards her.

'Thank you for leaving me alone with her,' he said briefly. 'Shall I wait here while you go back?'

'Yes, I...'

She stopped, realising that someone was hailing her from near the gate.

'It's him,' she said, pleased. 'It's Father Valetti.'

The father advanced, a big smile on his plump, youthful face, recognising her.

'I'm sorry I wasn't here,' he said. 'I've been at the bank. I'm afraid I'm not very good at finance.' He shook Rebecca's hand. 'I'm so glad you came back.'

'I always meant to, when the time was right. Father Valetti, this is Luca Montese.'

'The little girl's *papa*,' said the priest immediately, shaking Luca's hand. 'Have you been to see her?'

Luca nodded.

'And she does not seem quite real,' the father said. 'You think, what does this patch of earth have to do with my child? Especially after so long.'

Luca looked at him with sudden interest.

'Yes,' he said. 'That was exactly how it felt. It has been so long—I didn't know she was here.'

'But one day you were bound to come,' said Father Valetti gently. 'And she has waited for you.'

'I'm grateful to you for taking care of her. May I look round your church?'

'Of course. It will be my pleasure to show you.'

Rebecca slipped away to have a few moments alone with her daughter. When she returned the two men were deep in conversation, and she knew that Luca had discovered what she had discovered herself, that this was a good man, and easy to talk to.

He can talk to him, she thought sadly. *But not me.*

Luca smiled as he saw her, but he seemed abstracted, as though some thought was occupying him.

'What did you mean about the bank?' he asked the priest. 'Is the church in financial trouble?'

'We will be if I can't pay off the two-million loan I've just arranged,' Father Valetti said, with a weak attempt at humour.

'Two million euro?' Luca echoed. 'Is the church falling down?'

'Not the church. The money is for the new baby unit that we're building at the hospital. Costs are spiralling out of control, and without the loan we might have had to give up the work. It was my decision to sponsor that unit but, as I say, I have no gift for finance.' He grimaced. 'The archbishop is not pleased with me.'

'But you managed it?' Luca asked.

'On conditions. The bank wants guarantors, so now I must go around local businessmen asking each of them to guarantee part of the loan. And they all know what I want, and will run when I approach.'

'Then don't approach them,' Luca said.

'I don't understand.'

'I'll take care of it.'

'You mean you will guarantee the loan?'

'No, I mean you don't need a loan. I'll give you the money.'

Father Valetti looked doubtful, and Luca gave him a wry smile. 'It's all right, I have the money. I won't let you down. Will it be enough, or will the unit need more?'

'You can afford more?' the priest asked, wide-eyed.

Luca took out his cellphone and dialled Sonia.

'How long will it take to transfer three million euros?' he asked. 'Can you do it in twenty-four hours? Good. Then send it to this destination.'

He read out from a piece of paper that the priest hastily scribbled for him. When he hung up he spoke in a
hard voice.

'I'd like the baby unit named after my daughter.'

'Of course.'

'Rebecca Montese. Not Solway.'

'It shall be done. It is most generous—'

Luca shook his head to silence his thanks. 'Let me
know if you need more,' he said. He handed the priest
a card. 'This is my headquarters in Rome. That number
will get you through to my assistant, and she will call
me, any time. Are you ready to go?' This was to
Rebecca.

On the way home she struggled with her thoughts. She
wanted to thank him, but was checked by the feeling
that she had no right to. In a strange way his action had
had nothing to do with her. Luca had reclaimed his
daughter, but he'd done so alone, in a way that excluded
her.

Now she understood how much hope she had invested
in this moment. She had never realised that it could
strand her in limbo.

Why? she asked herself as they headed home in the
gathering dusk. Why had it happened like this? She had
thought they were travelling a road that would bring
them together, but she'd been deluding herself. Luca had
turned off abruptly onto another road where all could be
made well with money. He was, after all, a businessman,
and she had been foolish to forget it.

What price one daughter? Three million euros.
Signed, sealed and sorted.

You couldn't criticise a man who'd just endowed a
baby unit and potentially saved many lives. Not even if

you knew he'd bolted and barred his own heart in the process.

The cottage was still mercifully warm as they hurried in and settled determinedly into the domestic details, as though in them lay safety.

He did not speak during the meal, except to thank her. When she stole a look at his face she found it set like stone. Never once did she find him looking at her, or seeking in any way to reach out to her.

Darkness was falling as she went outside to collect more logs for the range. As she worked her mind was turning, making plans. She knew now that her future must be without Luca. He had dealt with this in his own way, and it could not be her way. He could not have made it plainer that he did not need her, and from now on their roads lay apart.

It was good that her love for him had died, and none of this hurt as much as it might once have done. She told herself this, and tried hard to believe it.

She had just finished piling logs in her arms, when she heard the first scream.

At first she couldn't imagine what it was, and stood listening. After a moment the scream came again, and then again. There was no doubt now that they were coming from inside the cottage. Dropping the logs, she began to run.

Luca was sitting where she'd left him, his hands on the table. His fists were clenched, but he wasn't punching this time, just leaning on them, his head down, while the sounds that came from him were those of a tormented animal. A bear, caught in an agonising steel trap, might have made those sounds.

On and on they went while she watched in horror. He seemed unable to stop.

'Luca—'

He straightened up and raised his fists to his head, covering his eyes, while the terrible howls went on.

It was ghastly, and worst of all was her realisation of her own stupidity. She had thought him unfeeling because he didn't speak of his emotions, but what he felt went too deep for that. He was telling her now, without words, that he suffered to the point of madness.

'Darling...' she whispered, putting her arms about him.

At once his own arms went around her, and he buried his face against her, clinging to her, as though there was nothing else in the world that could make him feel safe.

It had been bad enough when she first told him, and he'd punched the wall, but that was nothing. Today had come near to destroying him, and he was begging for her help in the only way he could.

'All these years,' he gasped, 'she's been alone—we never knew—'

'No, we never knew. But we won't let her be alone any more. Luca, Luca...'

She wanted to say a million things but now it was she who could not find words. She could only murmur his name over and over while she held him close, feeling his shoulders shake with the sobs that had been held in for fifteen years.

When, at last, the storm abated he leaned wearily against her, still trembling, but growing quieter.

'It just happened suddenly,' he said huskily. 'One moment I was coping, and the next I was engulfed in hell.'

'Yes, that's what happened to me. There's no defence against it. You have to feel it until it passes.'

'Does it pass?' he asked in a voice that tore her heart with its despair.

'In the end, yes. But you have to feel it first.'

'I can't do it alone.'

'You don't have to. I'm here. You're not alone.'

He looked up at her, his face ravaged and stained with tears.

'I'll be alone when you leave.'

She took his face between her hands and kissed him gently.

'Then I won't leave.'

At first he didn't react, as though she had said something too momentous to be true. Then he said,

'You don't mean that.'

'I can't leave you, Luca. I love you. I've always loved you, and I always will. We belong together.'

Very slowly he drew back a few inches, and laid his hand over her stomach, looking up with a question in his eyes.

'Yes,' she said. 'It's true.'

Silently he laid his face against her again, not trembling now, but finally at peace. When she took his hand he followed her into her room without protest.

CHAPTER TWELVE

As the first light came through the window Luca said softly,

'I thought you were never going to tell me that you were carrying our child.'

'How long have you known?'

'Almost at once. There was something about you—just like last time.'

'You can remember that?' she asked in a wondering voice.

'I remember everything about you, from the first moment we met.'

They had lain in each other's arms all night, sometimes talking, but mostly silent, seeking and finding consolation in each other's presence. As the minutes passed into hours she felt the shell about her heart crack and fall apart, releasing her from the imprisonment of years, and had known that it was the same with him.

'I guessed about the baby almost as soon as I saw you,' he said, 'but I couldn't see any hope for us then. I knew I'd made a mess of everything. You used to say I went at things like a bull at a gate, and it was true. I've gone on doing things that way all these years, because I could make it work for me. By the time we met again, I'd forgotten that there was any other way.'

'Yes,' she said tenderly. 'I gathered that.'

'When we were young I knew how to talk to you. It was easy to tell you that I loved you. There was nothing in the world but love, nothing that mattered. When we met again, there were so many other things that seemed important. Chiefly my pride.

'I sought you out because I'd convinced myself that you were the one woman in the world who could give me a child. It was nonsense, of course.

'Sonia saw it. She said at the start that I only believed it because I wanted it to be true, and she was right. So I came looking for you, convinced that I had a sensible, logical reason, because I couldn't admit the truth to myself.'

'And what was the truth?' Rebecca asked softly.

'That I'd never stopped loving you in all those years; that life without you was desolate and empty. All that time there was a barrier about my heart. I built it up year after year, thinking if it was thick enough it would protect me, but in the end it didn't, thank God.

'Then I found you, and I bought shares at the Allingham to give myself an excuse to meet you. I thought I'd planned it all so well.'

He gave a faint smile, aimed at himself. 'If you could have seen me on the night we met. I was almost sure you'd be at Steyne's house, and I was in a state of nerves. I heard your voice in the hall and I nearly panicked and ran. Then you came in with Jordan, and you were so beautiful, but so different, I didn't know what to say to you.

'I don't know what I expected—that'd you'd greet me by name, run into my arms? But you didn't seem to know me. You were so cool and poised and suddenly I was the country bumpkin again, fumbling for words.

'I tried to rush you—well, you remember that. But all I knew how to do was give orders, and you seemed to get further away with everything I said or did. I nearly blew it with those diamonds, but I couldn't think what else to do.'

'So you went at it bull-headed,' she said, smiling.

'As always. When I came here I'd given up all hope. I just wanted to look at the place where we'd been so happy. And when I saw you, I didn't dare believe that we might have another chance.'

He raised himself on his elbow, anxiously searching her face in the faint dawn light.

'We do have another chance, don't we?' he asked.

'We do if we want it.'

'I want nothing in the world but you.'

'And the baby,' she reminded him.

'Just you. The baby is a bonus. But the point of everything is you.'

He was asleep before she could answer, as though simply saying the words had brought him peace. All strain seemed to have drained away from him, as it had from her, and now she understood why.

For fifteen years they had been denied the right to grieve together for their child. That denial had been a disaster, freezing something in their hearts, preventing them both from moving on.

It was not too late, she thought, holding him close and watching the dawn grow. They were free now, free to feel the pain of their loss, and then free to grow beyond it, to find each other again.

She heard a faint pattering of rain on the roof. It became louder until she knew they were in the middle of a downpour.

It went on for several days, and during that time they never left the house. Some of the time they spent in talking, but mostly they just lay in each other's arms, beyond the need for words.

At last they made love, gently and tenderly. There was pleasure still, but it mattered less than the love they had found again, and at last he held her in his arms, whispering, 'Rebecca.'

'You called me Rebecca,' she said in wonder. 'Not Becky.'

'I've been doing so for some time. Have you not noticed?'

'Yes, I think I have,' she said, and fell asleep in his arms.

She had the strange, comforting fantasy that the water pouring down on the little house in a torrent was washing away all pain and bitterness. When the last of the storm had passed they went out together to look down the valley at the clean washed world.

'Breakfast,' she said.

Soon there were other things that would have to be said, but for the moment she wanted to think only of the small prosaic matters, and make this enchanted time last as long as possible.

'Breakfast,' he said, understanding her perfectly.

He helped her, fumbling slightly because of the plaster on his hand.

'I guess you won't get mad the next time I try to take care of you,' he said, waggling his fingers. 'I've never bullied you like you bullied me that day.'

'Some men need bullying,' she told him.

'Now, where did I hear that before? Oh, yes, it was what Mama used to say to Papa.'

'And what did he say?'

'Nothing. Just stood to attention.'

He suited the action to the words and she laughed. He grinned back, regarding her tenderly. There was a different quality to their laughter. It was no longer tense and brittle now that it was not being used to keep reality at bay.

One morning she opened her eyes slowly to find that, as always, the cottage was warm because Luca had risen earlier and built up the range. Pulling on her robe, she went out to find him bringing in a final load of logs; he dumped them in the basket, and blew on his hands.

Smiling, she went to him and took his hands between her own, trying to rub some warmth into them.

'That's lovely,' he said. Then, mischievously, he put his chilly fingers against her neck, and she shrieked.

'Sorry.' He grinned. 'It's just that your neck is so deliciously warm, and it's freezing out there.'

'Well, it's lovely in here.'

'And, as you will have observed, the kettle is boiling.' He indicated it with a flourish. 'If you'd care to sit down, it'll be ready for you in a moment.'

She let him enjoy himself cosseting her, but she was thoughtful, and he seemed to understand, because he was quiet until they were both eating.

'How are you feeling this morning?' he asked. 'Any sickness?'

'No, that's gone now, thank goodness.'

'But there is something on your mind, isn't there?'

'Yours too,' she agreed. 'I've felt it for the last few days.'

'I feel it every time I go in that cold yard. Winter's coming, and soon it'll be a lot colder.'

She nodded. 'It's been wonderful, being here like this, but I guess it's coming to an end.'

'It has to,' he agreed regretfully. 'Both for your sake and the baby's.'

'So what have you planned?'

'Nothing,' he said quickly. 'I was waiting for you to make suggestions.'

'You haven't arranged anything? You?'

'I may have had a few ideas—'

'I somehow thought you might have done,' she said, smiling.

'But they're only ideas. You may not like them, and then we could think of something else.'

Her lips twitched. 'You're making an awfully good stab at being "reticent man", Luca, but I can tell it's a struggle.'

'I'm doing my best, but I admit it doesn't come naturally.'

'Why not just abandon it and tell me what arrangements you've made?'

'They're not arrangements—not exactly. I only called my housekeeper in Rome, and told her to have the house ready—just in case.'

'Very sensible. You never know when you might decide to up sticks and go home.'

'But only if you want to. Would you rather go back to England?'

'Would you come with me?'

'Anywhere that's warm, as long as it isn't the Allingham.'

'No, I haven't got a home in England,' she said. 'There's nothing to go back to.'

'Then let's go forward. My house—it's never been a home, but you could make it one—'

'Let's take it one step at a time,' she said gently.

They started preparing for departure immediately after breakfast. It didn't take long. Luca doused the fire in the range while Rebecca gathered up food and took it outside to scatter for the birds. When she returned to the house he was waiting for her in the doorway, with her coat.

'Are we ready to leave?' he asked, helping her on with it.

'Just a moment. I want to...'

She didn't finish the sentence, but he seemed to understand because he stood back to let her pass inside.

There wasn't much to look around, just the bedroom where they had lain together truly united at last, and the kitchen where they had cooked and talked, and bickered, and rediscovered their lost treasure.

He came with her, not intruding but simply there, holding her hand, letting her know that their feelings were in harmony.

'We were happy here,' she whispered.

'Yes, we were—both times.'

'We will come back, won't we?'

'Whenever you want.'

'Then we can go now.'

With their few things packed into the car they drove back into the village, then he swung onto the road that would take them to Florence, and the *autostrada* that led to Rome. In Florence they stopped for lunch.

'You're not having regrets, are you?' she asked.

'No, of course not.'

'It's just that you're very quiet.'

'I was only thinking—'

'Yes,' she said. 'I've been thinking too. We're only

about twenty miles from Carenna. It wouldn't take very long.'

'Let's do it, then.'

Instead of heading straight for Rome he turned off onto a different road, and they were in Carenna in half an hour. At the church they found Father Valetti in the graveyard, heavily wrapped in scarves, deep in discussion with two men, with whom he seemed to be consulting plans. He hailed them with delight.

'Wonderful to see you. I didn't think you could have had my letter yet.'

'Letter?' Luca echoed. 'We've had no letter.'

'Then it's providence that sent you here just when I needed to talk to you.'

'Is something wrong?' Rebecca asked.

'Oh, no, not at all. It's just that in a tiny churchyard like this we always have trouble finding space, and graves don't last forever. Some of them receive few visitors after ten years, so it's normal practice to rebury those together in a smaller space, to make room for new occupants. But of course the families are always given the option of keeping the original grave for a fee. And I wrote to you to ask your wishes in this regard.'

'Do you mean,' asked Rebecca, 'that our baby is going to be raised?'

'She can be, but of course the coffin will be reinterred elsewhere with all respect.'

'Yes, but where?' Rebecca asked with a rising excitement.

'Well—'

'I mean, couldn't she come to Rome, with us?'

Luca turned on her quickly, his eyes alight.

'It might be possible,' Father Valetti said thoughtfully.

'Of course, it would have to be done in the proper form—lots of paperwork, I'm afraid. Come inside and let's look into it.'

In his office he sorted through forms while Rebecca and Luca sat holding hands, hardly daring to breathe in case their hopes had been raised only to be dashed.

'I'd need to know to which church she will be going,' he said at last, pushing papers across the desk at them, 'and the name of the priest who will conduct the ceremony.'

'I thought of having part of my own grounds consecrated,' Luca said, tense with hope, 'and keeping her with us.'

'Get the priest to send me official notification of the consecration, and I'll arrange the proper transport.'

'Then—it can be done?' Luca asked.

'Oh, yes, it can be done.'

Father Valetti was a tactful man, for he left them quickly. As soon as he was gone they turned to each other, speechless with emotions for which there were no words.

When at last Luca managed to speak, it was to say huskily, 'Thank you for thinking of this, my dearest.'

Rebecca rested her head on his shoulder and at once his hand came up to stroke her hair.

After a while they went out again into the churchyard and made their way quietly to the place where the little grave lay. Luca dropped to one knee, and laid his hand on the ground, looking intently at the spot.

Rebecca stayed back a little, guessing that what Luca wanted to say to his child was for themselves alone. Nor did she need to hear the words, for they echoed in her own heart.

'Be patient awhile longer, little one. Your mother and father are taking you home at last. And you will never be lonely again.'

When Luca had mentioned the grounds of his house Rebecca had somehow formed the impression of a very large garden. What she found was an extensive estate, partly covered with woodland.

It stood just outside Rome, on the Appian Way, a mansion, with more rooms than one man could possibly need. She didn't need his confirmation to know that it had been bought as a status symbol and chosen by Drusilla.

Despite this, there was no hint of Drusilla's presence, partly because she had stripped the place of all she could carry, and partly because, as Luca explained,

'We called it our home for lack of anything else to call it. But it was never a true home. We did not love each other, and there are no regrets.'

She knew instinctively that this was true, believing that a house where there had been love always carried traces of that love. Here there were no such traces. She and Luca could make of this home whatever they pleased.

He chose the brightest, sunniest room for the nursery, and decorated it himself in white and yellow.

'I'll paint pictures on the wall after the baby's born,' he said. 'When we know if it's a boy or a girl.'

'Have you thought about names?' she asked.

'Not really. At one time, if it was a girl I'd have wanted to call her Rebecca, after her mother. But now...'

'Now?' she urged. She wanted to hear him say it.

'We already have one daughter of that name. To have

two would be like saying the first one didn't count, and
I don't want to do that.'

She nodded, smiling at him tenderly. If there was one
thing above all others that made her heart reach out to
Luca it was his way of recognising their child as a real
person, who had lived, even if only for a short time, and
died with an identity.

'What was your mother's name?' she asked.

'Louisa.'

'Louisa if it's a girl, Bernardo if it's a boy.'

He did not reply in words, but his look showed his
gratitude.

'I think Bernardo Montese sounds good,' she mused.

But he shook his head. 'Bernardo Hanley.'

'What?'

He hesitated slightly before saying, 'Where the mother
is unmarried, the child takes her surname.'

'I don't like that idea.'

Luca took her hand and spoke gently. 'Neither do I,
Rebecca. But the decision is yours.'

They were married quietly, in the tiny local church.
Luca held her hand as though unwilling to risk letting
her go for a moment, and there was a calm intensity in
his manner that told her, better than any words, what
this day meant to him.

When the birth began he refused to leave her. It was
harder and longer than last time, but at last their son lay
in her arms, and she and her husband were closer than
they had ever been.

'You have your heir,' she told him, smiling.

But he shook his head.

'Labourers don't have heirs,' he said, as he had said
once before. 'It was a child that I wanted. Your child,

and nobody else's.' He touched her face. 'Now I have everything I want—well, except perhaps for one thing more.'

He had his wish in the spring when their daughter came home at last, and was laid in the spot he had chosen.

'I thought it would be nice here, surrounded by the trees,' he said to Rebecca when the service was over and they were alone. 'And there's plenty of room, do you see?'

She nodded, understanding.

'You don't mind?' he asked, a little anxiously.

'No, I'm glad you thought of it. But I want many years together first. We were apart for too long, and we have so much to make up.'

He kissed her hands and spoke with the same calm fervour as at their wedding.

'Years ago,' he said, 'two nights before we were to be married, I promised you that my heart, my love and my whole life belonged to you, and always would.

'Now I say it again. I will spend all my days making up to you for the suffering I couldn't prevent. And when life is over, nothing will change. Do you understand that? Nothing. For then I shall be with you forever, and that is all the world can hold for me.'

MILLS & BOON®

Live the emotion

OCTOBER 2003 HARDBACK TITLES

ROMANCE™

The Salvatore Marriage *Michelle Reid*	H5876	0 263 17771 8
The Christmas Marriage Mission *Helen Brooks*		
	H5877	0 263 17772 6
The Spaniard's Passion *Jane Porter*	H5878	0 263 17773 4
The Yuletide Engagement *Carole Mortimer*	H5879	0 263 17774 2
The Italian's Prince's Proposal *Susan Stephens*		
	H5880	0 263 17775 0
The Billionaire's Pregnant Mistress *Lucy Monroe*		
	H5881	0 263 17776 9
A Convenient Wife *Sara Wood*	H5882	0 263 17777 7
That Maddening Man *Debrah Morris*	H5883	0 263 17778 5
Outback Surrender *Margaret Way*	H5884	0 263 17779 3
The Italian's Baby *Lucy Gordon*	H5885	0 263 17780 7
The Wedding Wish *Ally Blake*	H5886	0 263 17781 5
A Bride for the Holidays *Renee Roszel*	H5887	0 263 17782 3
9 Out of 10 Women Can't Be Wrong *Cara Colter*		
	H5888	0 263 17783 1
The Nanny & Her Scrooge *DeAnna Talcott*	H5889	0 263 17784 X
A Very Special Christmas *Jessica Matthews*	H5890	0 263 17785 8
The Honourable Midwife *Lilian Darcy*	H5891	0 263 17786 6

HISTORICAL ROMANCE™

The Lord and the Mystery Lady *Georgina Devon*		
	H561	0 263 17837 4
The Chivalrous Rake *Elizabeth Rolls*	H562	0 263 17838 2

MEDICAL ROMANCE™

For Christmas, For Always *Caroline Anderson*		
	M479	0 263 17861 7
Consultant in Crisis *Alison Roberts*	M480	0 263 17862 5

0903 Gen Std HB

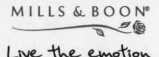

MILLS & BOON®

Live the emotion

OCTOBER 2003 LARGE PRINT TITLES

0903 Gen Std LP

MILLS & BOON®

Live the emotion

NOVEMBER 2003 HARDBACK TITLES

ROMANCE™

His Boardroom Mistress *Emma Darcy*	H5892	0 263 17787 4
The Blackmail Marriage *Penny Jordan*	H5893	0 263 17788 2
Their Secret Baby *Kate Walker*	H5894	0 263 17789 0
His Cinderella Mistress *Carole Mortimer*	H5895	0 263 17790 4
A Convenient Marriage *Maggie Cox*	H5896	0 263 17791 2
The Spaniard's Love-Child *Kim Lawrence*		
	H5897	0 263 17792 0
His Inconvenient Wife *Melanie Milburne*	H5898	0 263 17793 9
The Man with the Money *Arlene James*	H5899	0 263 17794 7
The Frenchman's Bride *Rebecca Winters*	H5900	0 263 17795 5
Her Royal Baby *Marion Lennox*	H5901	0 263 17796 3
Her Playboy Challenge *Barbara Hannay*	H5902	0 263 17797 1
Mission: Marriage *Hannah Bernard*	H5903	0 263 17798 X
The Marriage Clause *Karen Rose Smith*	H5904	0 263 17799 8
A Little Moonlighting *Raye Morgan*	H5905	0 263 17800 5
The Pregnant Surgeon *Jennifer Taylor*	H5906	0 263 17801 3
The Registrar's Wedding Wish *Lucy Clark*		
	H5907	0 263 17802 1

HISTORICAL ROMANCE™

The Unknown Wife *Mary Brendan*	H563	0 263 17839 0
A Damnable Rogue *Anne Herries*	H564	0 263 17840 4

MEDICAL ROMANCE™

Outback Marriage *Meredith Webber*	M481	0 263 17863 3
The Bush Doctor's Challenge *Carol Marinelli*		
	M482	0 263 17864 1

1003 Gen Std HB

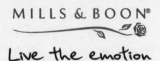

MILLS & BOON®

Live the emotion

NOVEMBER 2003 LARGE PRINT TITLES

ROMANCE™

The Frenchman's Love-Child *Lynne Graham*
1623 0 263 17947 8
One Night with the Sheikh *Penny Jordan* 1624 0 263 17948 6
The Borghese Bride *Sandra Marton* 1625 0 263 17949 4
The Alpha Male *Madeleine Ker* 1626 0 263 17950 8
Manhattan Merger *Rebecca Winters* 1627 0 263 17951 6
Contract Bride *Susan Fox* 1628 0 263 17952 4
The Blind-Date Proposal *Jessica Hart* 1629 0 263 17953 2
With This Baby... *Caroline Anderson* 1630 0 263 17954 0

HISTORICAL ROMANCE™

Wayward Widow *Nicola Cornick* 261 0 263 18007 7
My Lady's Dare *Gayle Wilson* 262 0 263 18008 5

MEDICAL ROMANCE™

To the Doctor: A Daughter *Marion Lennox* 485 0 263 18027 1
A Mother's Special Care *Jessica Matthews* 486 0 263 18028 X
Rescuing Dr MacAllister *Sarah Morgan* 487 0 263 18029 8
Dr Demetrius's Dilemma *Margaret Barker* 488 0 263 18030 1

1003 Gen Std LP